BR

Other Series by H.P. Mallory

Paranormal Women's Fiction Series:
Haven Hollow
Midlife Spirits
Midlife Mermaid

Paranormal Shifter Series:
Arctic Wolves

Paranormal Romance Series:
Underworld
Lily Harper
Dulcie O'Neil
Lucy Westenra

Paranormal Adventure Series:
Dungeon Raider
Chasing Demons

Detective SciFi Romance Series:
The Alaskan Detective

Academy Romance Series:
Ever Dark Academy

Reverse Harem Series:
Happily Never After
My Five Kings

BRIAR

Book 5 Of The Happily Never After Series

By

HP Mallory

10 Chosen Ones:

When a pall is cast upon the land,
Despair not, mortals,
For come forth heroes ten.
One in oceans deep,
One the flame shall keep,
One a fae,
One a cheat,
One shall poison grow,
One for death,
One for chaos,
One for control,
One shall pay a magic toll.

Briar:

Born of death,
Swathed in blood,
A rose in briar thorns,
Will lead a cursed legion to counter life's
callous scorn.

ONE
BRIAR

"Ouch!"

The sharp sting wrenches me out of the easy rhythm of the wheel and my pace falters. The pretty violet yarn curls in loops around my ankles. I'm hoping to have enough to make myself another blanket soon. The wind sweeps through the castle even on the mildest of days, chilling me. Maura says I'm frail, though I've never had the chance to test that assertion personally. I'm cloistered here in this castle and here I'll stay until some fickle prince decides to find me.

The color of the yarn soothes me, reminds me of Maura's eyes. She's often my only companion in this lonely place.

I stare forlornly from the tower window, hoping she'll arrive sometime soon. It's been almost a month since she was here last—when she brought me the faintly glowing orange stone and asked me to touch it. Once I'd

1

handed it back to her, she'd nodded sagely, as though I'd just proven something. Then she assumed her true form, flying away into the night without so much as a word to me.

After pricking myself another time on the spindle, I finally give up, pushing away from the wheel, letting my project fall by the wayside. It isn't as if it matters, really. Nothing is real here, anyway. Nothing but the shape on the bed or those slumped in the great hall and the guest rooms.

I cross over to the large bed and part the canopy, perching on the edge of the mattress, glowering at the huddled shape there. She curls into a ball in the dip in the middle of the mattress rarely, if ever, moving. The wavy, chestnut hair is nearly waist-length now and hopelessly tangled, even though she rarely stirs. I sometimes wonder if small imps crawl into the tower at night to play in those tresses.

Her skin is ashy pale, clinging to her bones. She's never eaten solid food and is only sustained by a spell and the potions Maura brings to keep her from wasting to nothing, a husk that somehow still contains a soul.

I prod her shoulder hard, though I doubt it registers at all through the thick down duvet and the ruffled nightdress she wears. The nightgown is much too small now. Maura doesn't always keep track of the girl's growth and hasn't given her another nightgown since she was fourteen. It barely touches her thighs now and strains taut across the bodice. Her breasts aren't extraordinarily large (or at least not as large as Maura's, which are the only measure I have for such things) but they are threatening to spill out of the top, all the same.

"Wake up," I mutter. "C'mon, Sleeping Beauty. You can do it. Let's get out of this castle."

"You know it doesn't work like that, lovely girl."

I whirl, a smile already stretching my lips at the familiar voice. I know who I'll see when I turn, but even so, she's so beautiful, I could weep.

Maura LeChance is perched on the window sill, blocking my view of the courtyard below and beyond that, the green sprawl of my kingdom. She's like a dark shadow against the moon. The silver light drapes over her body and face like a thin veil, outlining the bend and foreclaw of one leathery wing. If one looked at those alone, they might think she was a half-

3

shifted dragon. It's the rest of her, though, that banishes that thought entirely.

So far as I'm told, dragon females are rare. One born for every dozen or so males. They're prized as mates and kept secret, hidden beneath mountains like treasure. But, Maura's no dragon. She's too short, for one. Hardly any dragon women stand less than seven feet tall in their human forms. Maura's barely taller than me, and she says I'm on the smaller side, myself.

Maura is Unseelie Fae and she was once in line for the throne before she was usurped. It's the reason why she looks more human than most, with the exception of her wings, claws, and the curving ram's horns just above her ears. She's termed herself my faerie godmother, though that sort of thing is more of a Seelie tradition.

Her visage is more beloved to me than my own mother's at this point. Her skin is a dark brown that almost looks black, her hair springy and as dark as night, with spots of purest white in places. When she flies, it looks like her hair disappears into the night sky. Her eyes are violet, standing out startlingly from the rest of her.

4

"You're out of your mourning clothes!" I exclaim, taking in the red gown she's wearing.

In the whole time I've known her, she's worn black or navy dresses when she visits me in these dreams. Payne and his ilk killed many of my people before Maura had a chance to save me. She's been in mourning for twenty long years now. So… of course I have to wonder what's changed?

She smiles gently. "Yes, I am. I've come to deliver good news."

I eye her narrowly. "Good news?"

She nods. "I think I've found you a prince."

I take several steps forward and am just about to fling myself into her arms in pure joy, but I second-guess her words and make myself stumble.

"A prince?" I echo.

"Yes."

"But, it's been years, godmother! No one has gotten through the briars you've set up around the border of the castle. You said no one was worthy!"

She nods. "I'm still not sure he is worthy," she says with a shrug. "But, I'm convinced you're ready now, sweet Briar Rose. And at the rate he's moving, I believe he'll come to you three nights hence."

"Three nights?" I can barely believe it.

"If you wake, please accompany him to my tower. There are things we must discuss, and I don't wish to speak of them in a dream. They will only frighten you."

I'm shocked. I'm excited. I'm scared. I'm confused. "But…"

She reaches out one claw-tipped finger and presses it gently to my lips. "No, Briar. What do you say?"

I tuck my chin a fraction. "Yes, Godmother."

She smiles, exposing a pair of wickedly curved front incisors. She cursed the blood drinkers with those, as well, forcing them to find peace only when they took the blood of another creature. In life or death, they will never be wholly satisfied.

"Good girl." She pauses. "One more thing…"

I raise a brow. "Yes, Godmother?"

"When you see him…" She inhales, deeply. "Promise me something."

"Of course."

"Don't kill him," she pauses again, her smile growing a touch darker, her eyes glittering with malice. "At least... don't kill him *yet.*"

Kill him? How does she imagine I *would* kill him, had I the chance? And, furthermore, supposing I was capable of killing him, why would I want to?

She grins even more widely. "I'd like to watch."

And with that, she's gone, blinking out of my dream as if she'd never been.

I stare at the place she's disappeared in bewilderment. Who is this prince who is coming? And why in the name of Avernus would I want to kill him?

TWO
PAYNE
Days earlier...

I toss the limp body of the fox away with a sound of disgust. Animal blood tastes so vile, I can barely stomach it. Really the only thing worse are reptiles. Disgusting and often cold. I've eaten more than my share in the last twenty years. Why? Because there are no people in this wasteland any longer, all of them either killed during the Rose Castle massacre or shortly thereafter, when my retinue had been unleashed as a slavering horde of bloodthirsty beasts.

"We should rip out the throat of the Unseelie bitch when we find her," Tarquis mutters from my elbow. *"The magic in her blood ought to scrape the taste of beast from our mouths nicely."*

I glance dubiously at him. He's settled himself on a ridge of rock near my left elbow. Tarquis is my physical opposite in almost every respect. Short, where I am tall. Dark-haired

8

where I'm fair. Bearded, while I died clean-shaven. Brown eyes instead of blue. They're currently glaring daggers at the side of my face.

"We ought to move," he presses. *"Her tower has been visible for a week now, you little ponce. If we don't hurry, she'll disappear again."*

"There's no 'we'," I mutter. "You're a figment of my imagination, Tarquis."

Tarquis Mott was real once.

A friend and brother in arms who starved to death due to the dearth of animals in the kingdom. He and his brother Ruthven were the last of my retinue to survive, embracing final death almost five years ago. They were taken by a Shepherd, who'd been the only living soul in the place for years.

Now, I am a madman wandering alone, talking to an imaginary friend to keep myself from falling on a stake and ending things, once and for all.

The hunt for Maura LeChance had been the only thing keeping most of us going, in the end. A chance to end the dark Fae bitch who had cursed us all to this wretched existence. But finding her is another subject altogether. Her tower is cloaked and near impossible to find.

9

When it does reveal itself, it's almost always in an effort to make us expend the energy to find her, just before she disappears again. It's like a game and one that's beyond vexing, but I can't help myself. None of us can. We have to find a way to lift this curse.

"It doesn't matter what I am. Keep moving."

He's right. No matter how fruitless, I have to keep going. I'm closer to the tower now than I've ever been. So close, I can smell the char wafting off the armor inside. If I went at top speed, I might be able to touch the stones before Maura magicks the tower away again. But if I do that, I might run through my reserves more quickly, grinding myself into the cobblestone streets that much sooner. I refuse to die my final death before I've gotten a chance at ripping Maura's throat out.

So, I approach slowly, gripping the Fae-made sword I was gifted by my father almost forty years ago. I had just turned twenty and was expected to lead my troops just after my older brother died. I was given the sword in honor and I'd named it Bodach. Forged from Fae-metals and Unseelie blood, it was a

10

formidable and costly weapon. Proof of my father's trust in me.

I breathe in deeply as I remember the particulars. This is never a happy memory.

I'd failed him. Failed all my people, really. Failed myself.

Bodach hums softly as I enter the small courtyard arrayed around the tower. It's filled with broken, headless statues. It's rumored they were people once and that an old lover of Maura's turned them all to stone for a slight against her. Regardless, my blade can sense she's here. Blood calling to blood. The smell of char grows stronger.

If my heart were beating, it might thunder right out of my chest as this is the closest I've ever been allowed to the tower. Perhaps she's no longer inside and that's the reason why I'm being allowed to enter? Perhaps it's only her dragon lover within the walls. Even so, it's still a dangerous proposition.

I edge around the first statues, trying to approach stealthily.

Then a soft, female voice calls from an upper window;

"Come in, Payne. I've been expecting you."

11

Every muscle in my body bunches and locks down, stopping me dead. Of course, the fucking Fae witch knew I was coming! What did I fucking expect? There isn't much she doesn't know. But, if she knows I'm here, she must know what I've come for.

I lift my sword into a guard position before starting forward, still moving slowly. If she means to end me this night, she'll have to work for it. I've survived her wrath twenty years thus far and I don't intend to die the final death tonight.

The doorway is a square of inky darkness and even my keen eyes can't penetrate much into the gloom. I'm forced to sheath my sword after several feet. The corridor is narrow and there are many obstacles. Lumpy shapes that emit putrid odors. Corpses, in all likelihood. A false step and I could skewer myself on my own blade.

There's light at the end of the corridor and I use that faint prick of illumination to guide me, very deliberately not looking down. I'm not sure if I want to know whose bodies I'm stepping over. My comrades or the slaughtered members of the Rose family? Either will haunt me.

The hall leads to a set of spiraling stone steps, also clogged with bodies. I have to climb over the dead to reach my goal. I'm sure the Fae woman thinks the irony is just delicious.

I bring the blade up again the second I'm able, stepping into what looks like a bed chamber. It's hard to believe the lavish space belongs with the mundane stone exterior of the tower. Almost every spare inch is draped in some sort of luxurious material. Tapestries of pure gold of the sort my beloved Lelita had once made for me. Before she'd chosen that peasant boy to marry. Before she'd destroyed my hopes and dreams. Before she'd wrecked me.

I sweep a velvet swag hanging from one of the rafters to the side with a snarl. Bodach makes easy work of it, leaving the purple fabric in tatters. It's not as if there aren't enough of them to go around, in any case. The whole place is draped in shades of violet and gold, with the exception of its two occupants. Both lounge on the bed, curled beneath more velvet cloth. The woman—what I can see of her at least, is dressed in a gown the color of blood. It contrasts starkly with her dark skin and violet

eyes. She has one wing draped around her
bedmate, holding him to her breast.

The man looks quite content to be there.
He's her opposite. Broad where she's thin and
angular. Ivory-skinned with dark hair and a
square jaw lined with a day's worth of stubble.
His eyes are like coals flipped out of the grate.
Smoldering black with an edge of orange along
the outside. I'm told he's had seven sons but
only one of them looks or acts anything like
him... That would be the fearsome General
Malvolo.

His lips curl back away from sharp teeth
when he spots me near the door.

"Pluck his eyes out," Tarquis snarls in my
ear. *"Kill the scaly bastard and his Fae whore.
It's more than just... after what's been done to
our people!"*

"Now, Veles," Maura chides her lover
when he tries to sit up. She isn't paying
attention to me at the moment. Perhaps Tarquis
is right and I should strike. "Behave. You know
I've beckoned him here."

"Drop your weapon, vampire, or I will kill
you where you stand," Veles growls.

His deep, rumbling voice seems to have its
own gravitational pull. That might be exactly

right, in the end. Dragons only continue to grow larger as they age, with no cap on how immense their beast forms can become. If Veles is as old as he's rumored to be, he's got to be a massive fucking brute. I have to consciously keep my grip on Bodach as his will lashes against mine.

"Hush, my love," Maura scolds him, pressing him more firmly against one breast. "Don't think I can't make short work of the leech, should I wish."

Veles settles back against her chest, twining his long legs with hers, scowling at me but saying nothing more.

"Uxorious jacknape," Tarquis sneers silently at the dragon. I'm glad Tarquis isn't a real, flesh-and-blood construct or a ghost, as I've sometimes wished. If they can't hear him, he can't get us killed.

"If you're so certain of that, why run from us all this time?" I counter, hefting the sword into a defensive position, but making no move to attack the Fae or her lover.

Perhaps I'm not so eager for release as I pretend to be. I've never stepped into direct sunlight, thrust a stake through my heart, or thrown myself onto the holy symbols of my people. It'd be faster than a slow death by starvation and yet...

Maura throws the velvet coverlet off herself with a dramatic flourish, revealing the crimson gown is floor-length and... that Veles is wearing absolutely nothing except a scowl. It's difficult to keep my eyes on his face when his cock stands out so proudly between his legs. Gods! It's enormous! Can he club elk with the damned thing? I can't see how the petite and willowy Fae can accommodate such... girth!

She crosses over to me with a discordant laugh. It grates on my overly sensitive ears like claws drawn over slate.

"Running from you? No, arrogant little princeling. I was never frightened of your pack of baying beasts. I kept you running in circles so you wouldn't be drawn to the places where I moved *her*."

I instinctively know who she means, though she hasn't said the name.

Briar Rose.

The only known survivor of the Rose Castle Massacre, saved by the very Fae who stands before me. So far as I know, Princess Briar has been trapped in a death sleep for twenty years. I've never sought her, though Tarquis and the

16

others pressed for it. But I never could. Even my stomach can't handle seeing the dead shape of a babe laying on a dusty, abandoned cot. She wasn't meant to be targeted. Only that fucker Henry, whom Lelita had chosen over the alliance and our supposed love. I bore the child no ill will.

But Tarquis had.

The lack of support from our neighboring kingdom's troops had resulted in the sack of his parents' stronghold. His sister was killed in the attack. And, of course, he wanted vengeance. Vengeance which I granted, but that didn't mean the vengeance he sought went according to plan.

I should never have trusted him to simply poison the king and be done with it. That mistake brought on this curse. And it killed Tarquis, in the end.

"Kill the whelp," Tarquis snarls in my head. *"Take it all away from the Fae bitch!"*

"Then why let me in now?" I ask finally.

"Because you're the only one who can wake her." She grins that evil, knowing expression of hers and I fucking hate her even more than I did a second earlier. "True love's kiss."

I bark a laugh. "Love? I'm not her fucking love, LeChance. I killed her entire family. Do you truly think I can love or be loved by Briar Rose?"

Maura flicks a hand at me lazily and a gust of wind picks me up, slamming me hard into one of the stone walls of the tower. The golden tapestry barely cushions the blow. My back throbs somehow, though I don't understand how—usually I can't feel a damned thing, owing to my vampiric condition. Another flick of her wrist and I'm choking, blood burning up my throat, filling my lungs like a vase. Even though I no longer need to breathe, I still thrash, some leftover human part of me screaming that I can't live without air. My booted feet lash out at her as she approaches, trying to get some retaliation on the smug Fae bitch. She dodges me easily.

"I don't question the wisdom of forces greater than myself, Payne," she says. "Garrin says *you* are the one, so I will trust his judgment."

Garrin, the *limax mare aeternae*. A prophetic, god-like sea slug, whose mucus saved the babe Briar Rose. If what Maura says is true, I'm to wake the babe and then wait

18

celibate and starving another twenty-odd years while she grows to adulthood. Fat fucking chance.

"And what the fuck makes you think I want to cooperate with you, faerie?" I spit the words at her.

Her smile is as sharp-toothed and wicked as one of my own.

"Because if you assist Briar until her journey is through, I will lift your curse."

***

"They never fucking moved her!" Tarquis exclaims, almost as surprised by this development as I am. He's furious too, an emotion I'm struggling not to share.

Castle Rose stretches above us, a shadow of its former glory. There's been no upkeep on the red-stone fortress in over twenty years. It's faded to an almost salmon shade in the intervening years, due to constant exposure to the elements. The violent storms Maura LeChance drives through the kingdom prevent vegetation growing and thus, animal life, from thriving here. All in an effort to dwindle our numbers. We've been forced to scrape and

19

starve for two decades now. Because there's simply not enough blood to go around…

I'd never dreamed LeChance would keep her precious ward, Briar Rose, where the infant had been seen last. It seems pure insanity. But, according to the stone in my palm, the little brat is inside. The stone grows ever brighter the closer I draw to the castle. It seems to be some sort of magically-guided compass, leading me toward Castle Rose. Why the Fae woman couldn't have just told me where to find Briar Rose, I don't know. More games, no doubt.

I cross the drawbridge carefully, avoiding the bits where the wood has begun to rot and fall into the moat below. The rusted portcullis hangs like a set of dagger-like teeth over the entrance and I half expect the fangs to descend and scissor me in half. Luckily, it doesn't happen.

The interior of the castle is dusty and smells of old, moldering death. All the corpses lay in the precise positions they had before, undisturbed by human hands or animal scavengers. LeChance kept all predators out, including my brethren. After twenty years of damp, cold, and dark, they're mostly dried skin stretched over bone. No soft bits remain and even most of their hair is gone. It's difficult to tell who's who... the only conclusions I can draw happen to do with each corpse's social standing—owing to the finery of their clothing, or lack thereof.

Lelita and her farm boy, Henry, are still situated at the head of the table, hands linked together, heads bowed over their plates, dying too quickly from the deadly elixir to even release one another. The food on their plates has long since rotted away, but they're still present. At least, their bodies are. Still hauntingly real. Even if Lelita's blue satin dress has begun to degrade, her crown still glints in her fine chestnut hair, untarnished.

I can almost feel Maura's voice at my ear, whispering;

Look at it. This is all your doing, you monster.

I drop my gaze to the washed-out stones, unable to stand the sight for long. Not much can reach the cold, unbeating heart of Prince Payne, but this visual before me can. Lelita's betrayal cut me so deeply, my friends and I ravaged two kingdoms to get vengeance. I hadn't intended to kill her, her people, or her

21

babe. But I had, in a way, even if my hand hadn't administered the poison.

"Fuck Lelita," Tarquis scoffs, falling into step beside me as I make my way toward more sweeping staircases. The baby will be in a tower, no doubt. Princesses are always given towers, for whatever reason.

"Quiet, you," I mutter. "If I want your opinion, I'll ask for it."

He doesn't stop, of course. He's my only defense against encroaching madness if I haven't arrived at its doors already.

"We return the little brat to her godmother and we demand better food if she wants us to guard the winging thing. Hard to summon any feelings of true love on an empty stomach."

Tarquis is right about one thing at least. I *will* need better food. I can't drink from the babe, and the fox is the first mammal I've come across in weeks. If I can't feed, I will meet my end in another month. Perhaps less.

A spider, near the size of a rat, races along the curved wall as I pass and I briefly consider tracking it to the floor below. I've never had spider before, but most living things have blood. It would be something to bolster my strength for the return journey, at least. And,

22

perhaps, there are more inside the castle. For all I know, it could be a sanctuary for small animals fleeing the bloodthirsty creatures that prowl outside.

Later, I decide. I can track it once I've retrieved the princess and brought her to the lower level. Should I reunite her with her mother? Or would it be too morbid to place her inside her mother's arms? Probably.

The castle has seven levels and, of course, the princess' room is cloistered in the tallest tower. After what feels an eternity, I've performed so many corkscrewing revolutions, I feel vaguely nauseous and have to pause when I reach the very top.

The room beyond is almost bare, except for a spinning wheel in one corner, and a small table pressed to one wall. The table is covered in candles, all of them burned down to small nubs. The wax runs in rivulets off the table and pools on the floor. I can spy the imprint of a chair leg in one congealed puddle by the canopy bed. Maura has stood vigil here before.

There's a shape on the bed, mostly obscured by the gauzy canopy. Stalking forward quietly, I part the bed curtains. Stupid to do it with such care, because the figure

23

beneath the duvet isn't moving. Nothing, save for that enormous spider and myself, is moving in this blasted place.

I glance down at the person before me and freeze in place as I finally get a good look at her. Had I breath to take, it would surely stop at the sight of her. The amber glow of the stone highlights the planes of her face, the smooth fullness of her cheeks, the redness of her lips and the darkness of her lashes that matches the chestnut of her hair. This is certainly no winging babe.

"She's… she's a woman," I say, barely able to stop myself.

I'm struck dumb by her loveliness. *This* is Princess Briar Rose? I don't know how it's possible—that the princess has grown in these many years. I had expected to find her still a babe, caught in time and unchanged. I'd always assumed the death sleep froze her forever the way she'd been—an infant on the verge of asphyxiation. But she's become beautiful, despite her half-state.

She's the very image of my Lelita, with only a few things to spoil the illusion. Her hair is the same chestnut brown, though longer than Lelita ever allowed hers to be. The princess has

24

thick lashes that brush her high, sweeping cheekbones. A narrow, slightly snubbed nose she inherited from her peasant father. Full lips, and a slightly pointed chin that gives her face a heart shape.

This complicates things. Because Maura is right. I have a very good chance of falling for Briar Rose if she's anything like her mother.

And, yet, as soon as the princess awakens, she's going to hate me.

"That fucking bitch..." Tarquis mutters. *"She set us up!"*

I agree. Maura LeChance did set me up. She knew exactly what I would encounter here and she knew exactly how I would react. But there's nothing for it now. The only way out is to see this devil's bargain through—I will wake the princess and then take her on whatever journey Maura mentioned. Because if it means my curse being lifted from me...

I lean over the princess' prone form, rolling her to face me before I tip her chin up. She's cool to the touch, just like I am. The next best thing to dead, really. Not giving myself time to overthink things, I lean in and press my lips very gently to hers. They're soft, pliant, and still. I pull away again and look down at her in expectation of what comes next.

For a moment, nothing happens. And I wonder if I've not kissed her correctly? Perhaps it was too fleeting? Perhaps I am meant to keep my lips on hers?

Then her lips move, releasing a soft sigh of pleasure as her entire body comes alive. Or... more alive than it was just moments ago. She's still very cold but she's animate, at least. That's what matters. I can't explain why I do it, but I feel myself drawing closer to her again, wanting to taste those lips for a second time. And when our lips meet again, I revel in the feel of the silk slide of her lips beneath mine. She cups the side of my face then, runs her fingers across the smooth line of my jaw and darts her cool little tongue out to touch my upper lip.

And I'm shocked. Utterly so! More than that, my cock begins to stir, hardening within my trousers to such a point, it hurts. Twenty years and I haven't fucked any of my retinue, even the ones I could. I've simply... had no desire. But this woman—this princess who has been asleep for the majority of her life, suddenly has me hard in an instant.

Her eyelids flutter open and a pair of beautiful sage-green eyes locks with mine. She's frozen for a second, studying me in a way that says she's curious as to who I am, what is happening and why and yet, she's not afraid. She merely stares up at me and blinks a few times. I can't find the wherewithal to say anything and I just stare back down at her, instead.

Then lazy desire flees her gaze as understanding takes over. Recognition flares across her eyes and her lips tighten. The anger in her gaze solidifies into heated rage and Princess Briar Rose draws back a fist and slams it against my face.

THREE
BRIAR

I've long wondered what my first words would be when I am finally able to wake from this death sleep.

Maura says I was barely a month old when Payne's men came after my family. Not old enough to escape and certainly not old enough to articulate. Everything I know, I know so only because Maura has come into my dreams to teach me, to inform me. She's been my godmother, yes, but she's also been my tutor— teaching me the ways of the world and history, propriety and teaching me my subjects to ensure I become a learned woman when I do finally awaken. Even with all her illusions, I still feel woefully underprepared and unworldly. I've always pictured opening my eyes to a handsome prince and saying something along the lines of 'hello' or 'thank you'. A little mundane, maybe. But polite and sincere.

Yet, that's not what happened at all!

28

The prince who kissed me is handsome certainly. Tall and lean. There are hints of a muscled physique beneath his surcoat. I think it was a royal blue at some point, but it's so mottled with blood and filth, it looks black now. He's so pale, he almost appears to glow in the darkened interior of my tower room. His eyes are a perfect indigo, the shade so deep, I almost feel I could drown in them. They're nearly hidden beneath a fringe of golden hair. His lips are distractingly close, his cool breath still tickling my skin.

He's also familiar. And his familiarity surprises me, at the same time, it vexes me as I search to uncover our shared histories but come up empty-handed.

And then I remember. Then I understand. My godmother produced illusions of this man for me when I was very young, warning me against ever trusting him or his ilk. He's a vampire, one of the cursed blood-drinkers Maura punished for trying to kill me—for killing my family.

And he's just kissed me awake!

Suddenly, I want to scrub at my lips, spit, or cry. Instead, rage boils through me, heating me from the inside out so I feel truly alive for

29

the first time in my entire existence. My body is weak, my stomach is twisting itself into agonized knots, crying out for food, and there is a very large part of me that wants to sink back down into sleep again. Yet, there is another side. A side that boils with rage and sadness. A side that overflows with the need for vengeance. And that side wins. I ball one of my hands into a fist and lunge, striking him with the meager strength I have to offer, shouting;

"You fucking bastard!"

Well, my first words *were* sincere, after all.

Payne is scrambling off the bed before I get the chance to hit him again, which is a shame. It felt satisfying when the soft jelly of his eye gave slightly beneath my knuckles. I really can't summon the strength to sit up and follow. He backs into the only square of moonlight, either by happenstance or design, so that I can see him properly.

He's filthy, covered in mud and blood. Even his golden hair isn't immune, matted in places with the dried stuff. He clutches his eye, lips pulling away from his teeth to reveal glittering fangs. He makes a soft hissing sound like an angry cat.

"Now, what sort of greeting is that, Princess? I've come to wake you!"

"You tried to murder me!" I shriek at him. "Just as you did to my family! How dare you think to lay a finger on me! Maura will kill you and I shall laugh as you die!"

He lets out a low, pained chuckle sinking to the ground, getting his legs beneath him before he speaks.

"You'd rather have stayed asleep then?"

I don't respond. I simply glare at him as the breath heaves through my body and makes me feel quite light-headed.

"Don't blame *me* for this, Princess," Payne continues. "I'd have happily left you alone as I never wanted to return to this accursed place."

"Then why did you?" I insist.

He shrugs. "Your godmother sent me to rouse you. You want to hit someone? You should start with her."

My hands relax around the bedcovers, soft confusion sponging away the worst of my anger. Maura sent him to awaken me? But... No, that can't be right. Maura was sending me a prince! Payne must have eaten the true hero who was supposed to wake me! He must have... And then I remember Maura's words.

31

"Don't kill him. At least... don't kill him yet. I'd like to watch."

Oh Gods, she really *has* sent Payne to wake me! Why? Hasn't there been a single worthy prince in the twenty years I've been sleeping? Why him? Has Maura become so desperate to rouse me, she's dragged this filthy lout from the bottom of the barrel and thrust him at the problem, regardless of how I would feel about it?

Payne reads the dawning look of horror on my face and a wicked grin replaces his earlier irritation. There's something strangely compelling about his expression, no matter how hard I try to hate him. The danger those teeth present is oddly... intriguing. Sharp and as capable as inflicting pain as the spindle I constantly prick my finger on while spinning flax. I've never felt any sensation in my life outside of my dreams. Neither pain nor pleasure, hot nor cold, ecstasy nor despair. This is the first time I've felt... anything. And I'm not sure what to think about it.

"Good, you believe me."

Do I believe him? I suppose so because no other explanation seems to make any sense. "I believe you've done what you were meant to,"

I say with a scowl. I jab a finger at the door. It takes more effort than I could ever have dreamed to do it. What's wrong with me? I just feel so… exhausted. Yet, I've been sleeping all my life! Why am I so fatigued upon finally awakening? "Leave me," I say. "You've done what you were meant to do."

I crawl to the edge of the bed with great exertion and allow my legs to dangle over the side. My slippered feet meet the ground and I stand.

Or rather, I *try* to stand. The second my legs are forced to bear my weight, they fold and I hurtle toward the ground, flailing. I'd have cracked my head and put myself in another decades-long sleep if Payne hadn't darted to my side. He's monstrously fast, scooping me out of midair, hoisting my body aloft before I can hit the ground.

"Careful," he snaps, seemingly as uncomfortable with our close proximity as I am. "You aren't ready to walk yet."

"You don't tell me what to do!" I snap right back, anger burning me in a way that's all-consuming. "This is my castle and you're in my bedchamber! Now get out!"

"If I let you try to walk, you'll fall and knock your teeth loose, Princess," he answers with an easy smirk. "I can't collect on Maura's bargain if you kill yourself trying to get down the stairs."

A soft growl of frustration forms in my throat and furious tears prick in my eyes because he's right—much though I don't want to admit it. "Why can't I move?" I ask, not understanding what's happening to me. Have I been awakened just to start dying?

Payne chuckles. And the sound drives a flame into the fires that already burn deeply within me. I want to slap the self-impressed smile right off his decidedly kissable lips!

"Did you really think it would be that easy, Princess? You've been asleep your entire life! Your mind may know what to do, but your legs have never borne any weight, foolish girl! You're as good as taking your first steps!"

Gods! I'm like an infant even though I'm a fully grown woman. The prospect of having to train my body to move and eat? The thought instantly sours my mood even further. Can I control my own bodily functions? The thought of Payne trying to change my underthings is so mortifying, I could truly die.

My mind finally catches up to the latter half of his first statement and I frown hard, trying to stave off the tears I can feel coming. "Maura struck a bargain with *you?*" She cursed Payne and his people. I can't imagine she has need to barter with vampires…

"She did."

"And what was this bargain?"

He smiles again—and it's the smile the cat gave to the mouse, just before it pounced. "I'm to escort you on a journey. When you're through, Maura will lift the curse, thereby allowing me to resume my human form again."

"What is this journey?"

He shrugs. "I didn't ask and I don't truly care. So long as it gets me out of this damn kingdom. I'm so fucking tired of this place."

"You didn't think to ask where this journey would take you?" I demand, thinking it ridiculous of him. Unless, of course, he's lying to me.

"I didn't. Now, come along, Princess, I'll be your fucking chariot if need be."

Payne shifts my weight in his arms, easily gathering me up into a bridal-style carry that instantly has me irritated. I'm forced to loop my arms around his neck to stabilize myself.

Who in the name of Avernus does he think he is, waltzing in here like he's my intended? I want to storm away from him. But, of course, he's right. I can't walk. Yet, I also can't imagine him throwing me over his shoulder like a potato sack or lugging me around like a drunkard.

"Hold on tight," he advises, crossing the room in another too-fast movement.

We're at the door and then bounding down the steps like a ludicrous pair of jack rabbits. It's all I can do to hold on. Payne tugs me a little closer to his chest and I'm able to feel the hard planes of his muscles. I'm curious as to what his body looks like beneath his clothing, despite the festering anger. Regarding the male body and all its glory, all I've ever seen are the anatomical models Maura has shown me.

Yet, the reek of old death that clings to Payne tempers my ridiculous reaction to his nearness, reminding me he's a monster. A monster who's helping me, but a monster, nonetheless.

We emerge from the darkened stairwell and skid to a stop in a corridor. I crane my neck and lean out of Payne's arms. Maura said the castle was put under an enchanted sleep, much like I was. Will I recognize my mother with the new lines on her face? She must surely look different from Maura's memories of her? Perhaps I could wake her with a kiss, such as Payne woke me? Love comes in many forms, after all.

My hopes are immediately dashed when I spy a pair of shapes slumped at the base of a stone column. They wear surcoats, much like Payne, though these coats are red, instead of royal blue. Payne isn't wearing chain mail beneath his, nor full armor. I doubt he has need of it now that he's a night-stalking monster.

The shapes each have swords which are tarnished and lay uselessly at their sides. Mysterious stains crust the stones all around them, running into the mortar, staining it brown. There's nothing left of the bodies within but bone and the barest remnants of leathery skin.

They're not sleeping, at all. They're *dead.*

Does that mean...

"No," I whisper as horror dawns on me and my jaw drops open. "No, no, no, no, no..."

The weighty truth of it falls onto my shoulders, crushing every fragile dream I've had of reuniting with my family. There will be no reunion and there was never going to be one. If the guards are dead, it follows *everyone* is dead. Not only dead, but long dead, if the bodies are anything to go by.

A sob catches in my throat.

Mother. Father. Gone.

I will never be able to speak to them. And it's Payne's fault.

I hit him again, thrash and kick, using all the meager strength I have left to get the murderous bastard off me. Anywhere he touches me seems to crawl like maggots beneath dead flesh. He's a murderer and I don't want to feel him touching me.

One of my fists finally lands on its intended target, hitting him just under the jaw with enough force to momentarily stun him. And to stun myself.

His grip loosens and I roll out of his arms. The drop is higher than I expect and impact with the stone drives the air out of my lungs in a painful burst. My ribs protest the rough treatment, but I don't give them time to recover. I *have* to make it to the great hall before this monster drags me off by my hair, off to barter with Maura for humanity he doesn't deserve.

My hands form rigid claws and I drag myself forward, using the lines of mortar that divide the stone to propel myself. Foot by painful foot, I pull myself over rough stone until I reach the entryway to the great hall. I've seen it in its glory days, once again courtesy of Maura and the memories she was able to instill within me. Back then, this room was something boastful—with huge red and gold banners decorated with rosettes, the sigil of our house and my namesake. Mother made several of them herself. She was a genius weaver and a witch of considerable talent. And she was beautiful. Many men wanted her. Payne had. It was why he'd attacked, Maura said. To steal my mother from my father, King Henry.

A choked sound of denial trickles out of me as I take in the reality of the hall now. The banners are either in tatters, torn apart by hailstones that came through the highest windows, or else torn down by Payne's men. And what still remains of them have been tattered by time.

The long tables are still full of bodies, the fine china and silver sets, tankards and wine glasses still in place. Some of the bodies even have their hands clasped around their drink, the fingers splayed outward in their final, painful death throes.

But it's the pair at the head of the table that commands my attention. At first, it's difficult to tell them apart. Their corpses are both rotted past the point of recognizability. The skin clings like thin leather to their bones, their eyes are gone, their tongues rotted away, and even their hair is mostly gone. The figure on the right has wisps of wavy brown clinging to the base of her skull. Maura says I inherited my hair from my mother. It must be her.

Tears streak down my cheeks, hot and furious. Every muscle in my body clenches hard with denial. If I had a blade and the skill, I'd kill Payne this very instant.

Wake up, I will the skeletal figures. *This wasn't how it was supposed to happen! Get up, get up all of you! Get UP!*

Wind shrieks through the corridor, a frigid gale whipping my hair up and above my head. Icy fingers race along my body before being carried away by the wind. I can feel the cold settling into my bones. It's right to feel so cold. I'm alone in a cruel world with no one but a murderous monster to aid me.

Something attracts my attention—stops me from thinking another thought altogether. It's the bodies... the figures at the head of the table are... stirring. Slowly at first, and then with more vigor. They're moving.

I feel my heart start to pound in earnest as my brain attempts to make sense of what my eyes are currently reporting.

I don't know how it's possible. "Gods," I whisper as I watch every figure at the table begin to bend their arms, flex their fingers and some drop out of their seats. And then they're crawling, some of them pulling themselves to their feet, the sound of their bones scraping against the wood floors.

I feel sick to my stomach and suddenly even weaker than I did before. I feel my body collapsing against the floor as I'm even more overcome by the cold. Cold which is, little by little, taking the form of numbness, instead.

"What the bloody fuck?" Payne says in complete shock.

I'm not sure how they're moving without muscles or tendons. But after another few seconds, they're all standing. Then, in unison, every head turns to face me, as though awaiting orders.

"Fuck," Payne breathes out. "You're full of fucking surprises, aren't you, Princess?"

"Surprises?" I repeat, never taking my eyes off the newly animated skeletons before us.

"You're a fucking necromancer..."

I barely hear him.

Ringing sounds in my ears and my vision swims alarmingly. I close my eyes and take deep breaths, trying to cling to the thin fabric of reality to keep myself in the here and now. Bu fatigue drags me under, stifling the horror of the moment.

I embrace the blackness like a brother.

FOUR
PAYNE

"Now, look what you've done, halfwit! You've killed her!"

Tarquis paces a line behind me as I fill the stone depression in the queen's bedchambers with water. The thing was coated in dust and had to be cleaned of filth before I could place the princess in it. Most everything in the castle has been destroyed by the elements, but not this chamber. The spigot still appears to be connected to a well and will produce cold water if pumped. The princess would probably prefer warm, but we don't have time to boil it and then allow it cool. I'm also hoping the temperature will rouse her.

"She's not dead," I mutter.

I'm not entirely convinced of that. She's still and cold to the touch. I've touched the skin of her wrist and throat several times and I can't find her pulse. She's not breathing, either. But, still I'm not convinced...

43

"She's a necromancer," I assure myself. "I'm sure her body has the ability to reanimate itself."

A fucking necromancer!

Fate (or perhaps just a certain dark Fae) has a sick sense of humor. Of course, I'd be sent to rescue the princess with powers over the dead, and consequently, over me. Another way for Maura to punish me and keep me in line.

"And if she doesn't reanimate herself?" Tarquis counters.

I'm trying hard not to think about that. It's my hope the cold bath and the scrubbing I'm about to give her will bring her out of this fainting spell.

Her freshly shorn hair trails over the lip of the stone basin, tangled but looking distractingly touchable. I was forced to hack a good five or six inches off in order to get her here. The long, matted portions near the bottom kept tangling on every object we passed, jerking her head this way and that. I'm quite positive if she does awake, it will be with one hell of a headache. No doubt, she'll be pissed about her lighter head when she wakes, but we can't afford the liability at the moment.

Besides, it's not as though I can do much to fall even further in her estimation. I'm the man who murdered her entire family, intentionally or not. And then my retinue killed the rest of her kingdom in the first blood fugue. I can't do anything to change that history and I doubt she'll be inclined to forgive me for it. I'm the ruination of her entire world.

"She's dead," Tarquis says.

"She'll wake."

She has to. I have a bargain to uphold…

I lean half in the tub now, raising one of her arms in order to scrub it. There's dust on her clothes and tiny, muddy prints where a mouse or rat has scampered across her. It's difficult to keep my focus on scrubbing her pale, limp arm when her thin, white nightdress has become entirely translucent, giving me a very good idea of what lies beneath. She has surprisingly ample bosoms for someone so thin. She doesn't look too malnourished, which is probably the Fae's doing. The soft contours of her body are almost irresistible and it's all I can do to keep my would-be wayward hands on their proper path. I haven't had a woman in more than two decades. I'd stopped whoring when my betrothal to Lelita had been announced. Only to have my loyalty rewarded by a betrayal when she eloped with a peasant.

Tarquis reappears in the tub, leaning over the princess, phantom hands ghosting over her breasts, tweaking the hardened pink nipples. She doesn't react, of course. He's not truly there—just a ghost of my subconscious—a presence that appears to be growing more and more real as time passes. It's a thought that should concern me more than it does.

Instead, I seethe with jealousy as I watch him lean in, nuzzle his face into her neck, twin sets of fangs teasing her flesh. It's absurd to feel anything towards him. He's just a figment of my imagination, for the Gods' sakes.

"Take her. It'll be just like fucking Lelita, won't it? Turn her face away and you can't tell the difference. Her quim would be tight and wet in the bath and her blood sweet enough to…"

"No," I hiss. "I might be a monster, but I'm not a fucking rapist."

She can't stand me now. How much more would she hate me if she woke to me rutting her corpse-like body? Much though I desire her—I don't desire her like that. It's not right. I'll not stick my cock where it's not wanted. The only the way the princess will enjoy me inside her is if she asks me for it. And the chances of that happening are near impossible. Actually, they are impossible.

I've lathered, washed, and dried her hair by the time she wakes. I'm midway through braiding it out of her face, when she cranes her neck to stare blearily back at me. Then she groans.

"Apparently necromancy does quite a number on one's body," I grumble.

"So, it wasn't a nightmare?"

I chuckle. "No. I'm afraid not, Princess."

She breathes in deeply and then let's the air out. "I don't know… what to think about that," she says and eyes me then, scrutinizing every inch of me she can spy. "Why aren't you wearing any clothing?"

She sounds a touch panicked when she asks. Maybe she's wondering if I'm about to do what Tarquis has been urging me to this whole time.

"I thought we both could use a bath."

"Both of us?" she repeats, sounding appalled.

"The towel is covering my cock, Princess. Don't worry. Your poor virgin eyes are quite safe."

47

Her eyes flick down to my lap. She can't seem to help it. I'm tempted to draw the towel back to see if her eyes will bug… and to see if she might like what I have to offer. But, then I catch myself and remember the situation I'm in.

"I bathed. I scrubbed myself clean before doing the same to you. I figured you want to look nice when you meet your faerie godmother for the first time. And… I thought it might wake you." I smile broadly. "And look, I was quite correct."

She startles, sloshing water out of the bath and onto the floor. Her hands fly to her front and the look of outrage on her face dims only a fraction when she finds herself still dressed. Not that it does her much good. I have a pretty good idea of what her body looks like beneath it.

"You could have let me do it myself!"

"You were quite passed out, or don't I need to remind you?"

"You could have waited until I woke up!"

"As I mentioned earlier," I respond in a dry tone. "I thought it might help to *aid* in your waking."

"I think that sounds like quite a bit of hogwash!"

I frown at her. "You were literally dead to the world for an hour and a half, Princess. I was prepared to bring your washed and perfumed corpse to the faerie if I had to."

She stares at me. "You... you really don't give a damn about anything, do you?"

Her question surprises me. Possibly because I wasn't aware I've been so predictable. "I haven't for a long time. Only one thing matters to me and that's getting the fuck out of here."

"Out of here?" she repeats.

"This fucking kingdom. I haven't heard a word from the rest of Fantasia for twenty years."

"Then... we are the only living people here?" she asks, but I'm quite certain she already knows the answer to that question.

"We're the last two souls for miles, Princess."

"Briar."

"Pardon?"

She chews on her bottom lip. It's fucking distracting. I want to tear it open with my teeth and suckle the blood, taste her as thoroughly as I can. She's a siren's song to my newly awakened libido. My cock is hard and makes a very visible bulge against the towel. She doesn't seem to notice this time.

"Call me Briar. I don't like the way you use my title."

"How do I use your title?" I demand.

She shrugs. "Like it's an insult. And, really, what sort of princess am I?" she continues as she sighs and looks around the room. "It's not as if I have anyone to rule over anyway."

True. "Fine. Are you ready to get out of the damn bath, Briar? I'd like to be off. There's clothing laid out for you beside the tub. If I lift you out, can you dress yourself, or do I need to strip you down?"

At last, color flushes into the waxy skin of her cheeks, a faint dusting of pink.

"I'll manage."

A pity. I'd have liked a good excuse to touch her more intimately. But as I said to Tarquis, I'm not a rapist and I never have been. Prince Payne has never had to resort to forcing women into his bed. I smile thinly at her.

"If my *Princess* commands," I say, backing out the door of the washroom and into the queen's chamber. I barely dodge a very dusty cake of soap she lobs at my head.

"Arrogant fucker," she mutters to herself. My smile grows. A foul-mouthed princess. That's at least a novelty.

You have no idea, Briar, I think. *You have no idea.*

FIVE
BRIAR

I can't stop dying.

We've been traveling together for three days and I can't seem to stop dropping dead at regular intervals. At first, Payne thought it was a little funny and compared me to a woman he'd once known who was likely to drop off to sleep many times in one day. He teasingly called my condition 'necrcolepsy'.

Not that I ever thought his jokes particularly funny, but the situation even dawned on him that they were far from when, during one instance, I tipped toward the fire, almost burning another inch off my hair. And again, when we were stopped by a stream, and I fell in. He'd been forced to swim a mile to catch me in the fast-moving current. That was when Prince Payne lost his sense of humor where my recurring deaths were concerned.

I never stayed dead for more than ten minutes or so, but it was clear it was a problem.

I wake in Payne's lap this time, with the branches of a pine towering high above me. The winds are fierce outside the castle and I find myself in a rain of sharply scented needles. I splutter and have to spit several out. Payne tucks his chin so he can look at me. His expression is a little distant, like I've pulled him from deep thought with my choking fit. He idly brushes the needles from my face and hair.

The contact sends little jolts of sensation through me. I'm not sure if it's owing to my long sleep, but my skin reacts to his touch violently. It feels hot, and I feel flushed all over, my freshly beating heart speeding, and my lips tingling with the memory of his mouth on mine. I want him to do it again. Which is idiotic. He's a killer and more than just that, he's a bloodsucker. An undead. A true monster. Not to mention the number he did on my family! To hear him tell it, every guest at the wedding was poisoned by one of his men. That included me, an infant no more than a month old. What sort of monster kills infants?

This one.

And that's the reason I'm able to ignore my twitching fingers. I *won't* lean up and brush my lips along his jaw. I *won't* edge my fingers under one of the shirts he stole from the castle. I *won't* ask him to touch me in return. I can't let him get into my head like this. He's a glorified bodyguard at best, not some sweeping romantic hero. And he's not even really a bodyguard. He's more a bounty hunter, doing what he must in order to collect his prize—the removal of his curse. It's not like he's here willingly. He's been drafted by my godmother.

"You're back," he says mildly. "This episode was longer than the others. I think your death spells are getting worse."

"Maura will know what to do."

"If you make it that far."

I look up at him and frown. "What do you mean?"

He shrugs. "I mean we still have another day's journey. It's not as if I can go my top speed while carrying you. Any second, you might drop dead. And what if the next time is forever?"

"Why would you think it would be any different than what we've already seen?"

He shrugs again. "Because your little death spells are lasting longer each time." He shakes his head and frowns down at me. "I can well imagine the welcome I'll get from LeChance and her dragon lover if I turn up with your supposed corpse. He'd probably rend me to pieces."

"Which would be quite an improvement, if I do say so…"

"Ha ha, princess, very funny."

"Briar."

But he's not listening. Instead, he's in his own thoughts, even though his mouth is still going. "And then there's the matter if she *can't.*"

"Can't what?"

"Can't pull you out of your death sleep or can't make it stop," he answers.

"Why wouldn't she be able to do either? She's Maura LeChance!"

"Doesn't matter who she is," he answers with the expression of someone unconcerned.

"What do you suggest then?" I snap. "You sound like you're leading this conversation in a certain direction."

He smiles at me—that grin that says he knows something I don't. And it's just as frustrating as he is. "You are quick."

"Answer the question."

"I suggest a bond."

"A… what?"

"I've been thinking hard about it for the last day and a half and it's the only thing that makes sense."

He'll have to explain the logic to me then, because he's the only one it makes sense to. "What in the name of Avernus are you on about?"

He leans closer to me and I let him, even as I'm surprised my instinct isn't to pull away. It's almost as if my body trusts him. As ridiculous as that sounds because I can't trust Payne for anything. Regardless, his hand skims down my cheek and down the column of my throat to the spot where my pulse throbs. His eyes fade from indigo to ruby as he eyes the pulse point. I've only seen that look once, when he set on an enormous spider in the castle. And ate it, making a face all the while. Apparently, there wasn't much blood.

Regardless, his expression now is primal, an unstoppable hunger and now, I'm its focus. I should edge away from him, but there's no use. I can barely walk unaided. I certainly can't run from him. If he's going to give into his blood lust and kill me, there's nothing I can do to stop him.

But, he doesn't. At least, not yet.

"A blood bond," he says, the patience in his tone belying the desire in his eyes.

"And what is a blood bond?"

"Well, I've never done it before and I've only ever seen it done between vampires but I think that maybe... I think we're close enough."

"Us?" I demand with a laugh. "Can you please explain to me how you and I are close at all?"

"As far as our species," he insists.

"On that count, as well! You and I have nothing in common!"

"There you're wrong," he says and gives me that serpent smile. "You're at least half-dead and you practice death magic so..."

I'm not sure I agree with his announcement that I'm 'half-dead', but I decide not to argue. "So what?"

He licks his lips, eyes narrowing on me. "I've seen my kind bond by sharing their blood."

"Both are vampires though?"

He nods. "Yes, a blood bond between vampires."

"And what does it do for them?"

"They become better at cooperation on a hunt. One can lend the other life energy when they should fall injured or starve. It's how Tarquis and Barclay stayed alive as long as they did."

"What does that have to do with me?"

"You aren't a very smart girl, are you?" he asks as he frowns over at me.

"I'm a woman!" I insist, thinking it odd that such is the remark I decide to defend.

He chuckles. "I believe if I lend you my strength, you may be able to walk unaided and only die when I do… for the day."

Sharing his blood sounds revolting, but maybe he's correct. Something has to change. At the rate we're going, I won't make it much further. Now that I'm alive again, so to speak, the thought of slipping back into my comatose state is terrifying. But the question remains: am I willing to tie myself to my parents' murderer for a chance at life?

The honest answer makes me want to lean over and vomit on his shoes.

Yes.

Yes, I am.

It doesn't even take much thought. I simply *cannot* live like that—shut up in a castle with no other living souls. Only the corpses of a family that hasn't been mine in years. I won't shut my eyes forever and miss out on a chance at life, real life. Even if Payne and I are tied together, it doesn't mean we have to like each other. He said nothing about the bond being romantic in nature. After all, two men entered into a bond with one another. Unless they both liked men... well, even then. I don't have to act on any... feelings that might occur.

"How do we do it?" I ask.

Something like a relieved sigh breezes from his lips and he resists a smile. "It's fairly simple. I bite you, take your blood, and give you some of mine, in return."

My stomach rolls again. It still sounds disgusting. "Are we going to do it now?"

He raises a brow at me. "Do you see any reason to wait?"

He has a point. My next swallow feels like I've downed a mouthful of glass. I can practically taste blood already, my throat is so dry.

"Do it."

He doesn't have to be told twice.

Payne lifts me from his lap, arranging me so we're facing one another. I swear he's breathing faster—well, if he had a working respiratory system, that is. If he had a heartbeat, would it be galloping like mine?

"Arms around my neck, Princess."

"Briar," I remind him.

"Briar," he amends. "Hold onto me. If it hurts, scratch or bite the ever-living fuck out of me to take your mind off it. I won't hold it against you."

"Wait… it's going to hurt?"

He chuckles. "Well, what did you think someone biting you was going to feel like?"

I glare at him. "I like how you conveniently forgot to include that detail until I'd already agreed."

He smiles, long and wide.

And how much I hate him in that very moment! This was his moronic idea and he's the reason I'm in this position in the first place. If he hadn't killed my family and gotten himself cursed, he'd be in his forties. Likely married with a few children my age. That thought cools the desire stirring in my belly and allows me to steady my breathing. This is a business transaction. Nothing more. A little bit of pain and embarrassment for a measure of independence later.

I lace my fingers at the nape of his neck, resisting the urge to play with the hair that tickles my fingers. It's surprisingly soft, now that he's washed the blood from it. He hauls me closer, pressing our bodies together so I can feel every hard muscle through his shirt. And I can feel something else is hard too. How? He doesn't have a heartbeat to make the thing... work, right?

Wrong. Very, very wrong.

Payne's lips press to the hollow beneath my ear first, a brush so soft, I could have mistaken it for butterfly's wings. His next kiss is a little firmer and then he surprises me by latching onto my earlobe, rolling between his teeth just hard enough to make my hips jerk into his. My pelvis performs an instinctive little roll as the desire unfurls anew.

"Stop," I breathe. "We agreed… Just bite me and nothing… nothing more."

He laughs, his soft breath feathering over my face. He laughs like he knows what I truly want—more. His breath doesn't smell of death. It's sharp and clear, like pine. He must have chewed a few of the spiny leaves while I slept, just so his breath wouldn't be objectionable to me.

"Killjoy."

His lips move to my throat again, trailing down, leaving cool, sticky kisses on my skin. He pauses, then licks me, tasting my pulse before he drives his fangs into my neck. I yelp instinctively but then, a moment later, the pain is gone. Something warm trickles into my veins, numbing all feeling an instant later. It feels heady, the way drunkenness always sounded in the stories Maura read to me.

"You said it would hurt," I groan.

He pulls away and looks down at me. "I was testing your courage."

I glare at him and he chuckles. "Are you done?"

"No, I've only just begun."

And then he's back on my neck, sucking and drinking me and that numbness takes over again. My brain fogs, filled only with a warm sense of pleasure. My hips buck into his again and this time his cock drags along the front of my sex, thick and ready. It would be easy for him to tear my small clothes away and sheathe himself inside me.

Why can't I find that a distressing notion at the moment?

He moans against my throat and then the suction really begins in earnest. His hands are hard and eager on my body, holding me in place. Even if I had the will, I don't think I'd have the strength to pull away from him. He swallows fast, making pleased sounds as my blood seeps into him.

And then it's over. He pulls himself away from me—just enough for me to get a good look at him. He licks his lips, clearing away the crimson stain of my blood. He drags his bottom lip between his fangs, cutting it to ribbons, streams of bright red blood emerging from the wound. And then his mouth is on me.

The kiss steals my breath. His lips are hard, urgent, and hungry. I can't deny an answering hunger in myself. I've never been touched by a man. My skin craves his touch like the earth craves rain. I need the contact. I moan into his mouth and he presses his advantage. His tongue delves into my mouth and I taste pine and the metallic tang of blood. I can't even find it in myself to feel repulsion at the coppery taste.

Strength floods my body in another heady rush, my fatigue banished completely. I feel like I could run miles!

Payne lifts me off his lap and in the next second, I'm on my back before the fire, with Payne settling himself between my thighs. His weight above me is welcome and more than a little thrilling. He's still kissing me. I reach for the buttons on his shirt instinctively, as if I've done so numerous times before. And then...

It hits me again.

This man is a killer.

A jealous, callous bastard who slaughtered a nation because he couldn't have the one he wanted. He must fucking love this. Briar Rose, the spitting image of Lelita Rose, his long-dead love. And now he can tether her more agreeable daughter to him forever.

With my newfound strength, I push him off me. He rolls and has to contort his body to keep himself out of the fire. He looks dazed like a sleepwalker just woken.

I won't let myself be used by this man! Not as a stand-in for my mother. Not as his way to break a curse. I need him, for now. But when he delivers me to Maura, I want her to kill him. This dangerous man can't be allowed to purloin a part of my heart. Ever.

"We were just getting to the good bits," he starts.

"I'm not her," I spit at him.

"What?"

"I'm not my mother."

"I know that," he says defensively. There's a flinching around his eyes that makes me distrust the sincerity of the statement.

"No," I mutter. "I don't think you do. And that's why I want to sleep… on my own tonight."

I climb to my feet, relieved when I don't fall dead. I'm a little shaky, but I think given time, I'll be able to walk without stumbling. Perhaps even run.

Then I sidle into the night, away from my bloodthirsty companion, to sort out the problems that lie ahead.

SIX
PAYNE

The taste of her still coats the back of my tongue, taunting me, driving me mad every time I swallow. She's the sweetest thing I can remember tasting in either life. Sweeter than honey, sweeter than the first taste of blood after the change. The magic she possesses is staggering and it felt like trying to swallow pure moonlight. It was more than mere feeding. It was a revelation. More exhilarating than a chase, more potent than the best fuck I've ever had.

I can't stop staring at her, though I get a tongue lashing every time she catches me looking. She's right. She's not her mother. She's something new and incredible. Maybe it's the blood bond, but I'm drawn to her irresistibly, craving her more every day. Her blood, her body, her... everything, really.

"As if she will ever let you fuck her," Tarquis sneers. *"You're delusional, Payne. Find a whore the second we're out of this*

godsforsaken place. Fuck her and then rip her throat out."

Some part of me cringes away from the idea.

Killing has been a necessity for so long, it's almost become ubiquitous. I no longer want that to be my reality though. An attempted assassination started this mess and I'm loathe to continue the vicious cycle. Not only because Maura will probably find something unspeakably awful to inflict on me if I continue to slaughter innocents, but because I no longer want to be *that* man. I thirst for blood, yes, but if I'm ever to escape this constant hungering need within me, I have to act... well... human.

"Milksop."

"Go away, Tarquis," I mutter.

He grimaces, but finally vanishes from my sight, gone for now. It's getting easier to ignore him as we travel. He comes out when my blood lust is high or my need for *her* grows too great. Odd that the avatar for my base urges is warning me away from her. Maybe my hindbrain is smarter than the rest of me. It knows she'll probably get me killed.

I can't scrounge up an ounce of worry to fling at the idea. My mind is too focused on watching her. She's breathtaking in her mother's hunting attire. She finds it easier to move in the riding attire than the dresses she ought to be wearing. A short saxe skirt that rides up almost every step, woolen tights to keep the ensemble modest, and calf-high leather boots. A well-cut creme jacket completes the look. The long sleeves keep the cold off her. Mostly. Her nipples still strain the fabric of the teal shirt.

She's caught me looking again. Damn it.

Her face creases in a scowl as she glowers at me.

"Stop it."

"You're walking ahead of me. I can't not look at you."

"Oh, bollocks, Payne. You know exactly what you're doing. You're a scoundrel." I suppose a scoundrel is better than a monster. Perhaps I'm moving up in the world.

"And what exactly is it I'm doing, dear Princess?" I snap, my temper getting the better of me. Tarquis' disembodied snicker sounds in my ears.

"You're comparing me to my mother again."

I stop in my tracks, feet sliding in the muck. The grass has all but eroded from the hill, scraped raw by the almost constant pounding of rain or hail Maura sends to torment me. Maura's tower is within running distance now. No doubt Veles is observing our approach. We should be moving so we can reach the tower before dawn. But I can't take her antagonism for a moment longer. Not to mention the fact that she's completely wrong.

I return her glower. "I wasn't comparing you to your mother."

"Oh, then what were you doing?" she insists, her eyes narrowed.

"Do you really want to know?"

"Yes!"

"I was staring at your ass and wondering what your quim tastes like."

And the words drop the knowing expression right off her face. I chuckle. I can't help it.

"Well, I…" she starts.

"You what?"

"I…" but she can't say another word, possibly because her face is bright red and she's clearly completely embarrassed.

"I can look at you if I damn well please and it has nothing to do with what was between your mother and me."

And that's when she loses her expression of shock and a knowing glare takes its place. "There was nothing between you and my mother."

"Bullshit."

"Maura told me…"

"Only what it would take to poison your mind to the truth."

She crosses her arms beneath her ample bosom. It's distracting, to say the least. It hoists her breasts at least a few inches, creating a deep line of cleavage I'd love to bury my face in.

"Oh. So you *didn't* murder my family?"

"I only meant to murder your father."

"Only meant?" she shrieks at me. "And yet you poisoned the entire kingdom!"

I shake my head. "The poison administered was supposed to mimic a slow, wasting disease. For your father only. No one would have known it wasn't natural causes."

She barks a short, humorless laugh. "Oh yes, because that's so much better."

"It *would* have been better. I didn't want everyone to die, least of all, your mother."

70

"You arrogant, self-obsessed bastard! No wonder my mother hated you! You are the most vile, horrid creature to ever walk this land!"

A snarl builds and slides out through my bared teeth. It's as feral as a wolf's and it sends her skittering back before she can stop herself.

"I was thinking of my people! Your mother was a royal. She had duties! Without the alliance with her kingdom, half my people were slaughtered. Innocents brutally cut down because *she* decided to choose love over duty. I needed her troops to stop a war and stop the suffering. Our marriage was one that was meant to save my people!"

"You wanted her," she starts and I interrupt.

"Yes, I wanted her! But I prized her political might over her body, Briar. A traitor in my camp swapped the poisons." I take a pause as I realize the futility of this conversation. It doesn't matter what I say because the outcome still remains the same. Everyone in her kingdom is dead, owing to me. "Now none of it matters. Everyone is dead but you and me. So, you can sneer at me all you like, princess. I don't give a damn. I just tried to do what I thought best at the time."

Briar stares at me for several long, stunned seconds. When she speaks, her tone is softer, a little uncertain.

"Maura didn't tell me any of that."

I snort. "Of course she didn't because it might have made my actions a bit more understandable."

"You still wanted to kill a man—a man who didn't deserve to die."

"That's true," I say with a quick nod. "But, in that case, I believed the good of the many superseded the good of the one. And as to Maura… the Unseelie love their lies. You want trustworthy counsel from a Fae, try the Seelie. They're a bunch of pretentious bastards, but they'll give you truth. Cutting candor, but true honesty nonetheless."

We begin moving again and she trains her eyes on the muddy path, like the scant vegetation has suddenly become fascinating. She doesn't say a word until we reach the very edge of the courtyard, with its many headless, granite statues.

"I'm sorry," she whispers.

"For what?"

"For not knowing the whole situation. For accusing you of killing my entire kingdom in cold blood. I understand… more now. I mean, I understand why you thought of your people. I still think you made the wrong move, no matter what. You had no right to try to kill even my father. But I am sorry for the loss of your people. I imagine it must be difficult."

She continues moving, not looking at me, and I'm left staring at her back as she disappears into the darkened doorway of the tower. An apology? From one of the Royal House of Rose? I stumble, feeling like I've just been concussed. I never thought to hear an apology from any of them, least of all her. And I can't say I deserve it. I don't. Because she's right—I had no right to do any of the things I did.

She won't be able to ever forgive me. Understandable. But it's progress. I'll take less hostile if that's all she can manage.

I finally shake the shock off long enough to sprint forward, covering the distance quickly so that I'm hovering near her shoulder as we walk. I don't trust the Unseelie bitch around her, even if she saved the girl, once upon a time. The Unseelie don't do things without ulterior motives.

The trip up the stairs treats me to another glorious display of her ass and hips as she moves purposely upward. She's a little thin from her years of inaction, but with a steady diet, I'm sure she'll fill out into the fulsome figure she's destined to have.

We emerge into the tower room, though it takes me a moment to be sure we haven't somehow arrived in the wrong place. The room has completely rearranged itself. There are still the swags of rich fabric and some of Lelita's tapestries, but that's the only commonality. The room now sports a hearth on one side of the room, a large bearskin rug across the stone floor and a number of cozy armchairs, two of them occupied. Veles has deigned to put on trousers for the meeting, but he still looks almost indecent. He's got muscles a carnival strongman would envy, gleaming with sweat, which only draws attention to them. He smirks unrepentantly when he catches both Briar and I looking.

The fire in the grate burns green, Fae fire, which burns hotter than mortal flame. Briar shrugs out of her coat at once and I'm tempted to remove the surcoat. It would only leave me in a thin shirt and trousers. I don't strip, because I don't want to vex Briar again today.

Briar spots her godmother lounging catlike in one of the chairs and her entire face lights up. The first true smile I've ever seen graces her lips and she practically hurls herself across the room into Maura's waiting arms. The Fae smiles back, though the expression looks unintentionally sinister on her face. Force of habit, probably.

"Maura! Oh, Maura, thank you, thank you, thank you!"

I'm tempted to grumble at the effusive praise. It's misdirected, isn't it? I'd been the one to kiss her awake. Not to mention, I'm also the one depleting my reserves by lending her my strength day after day.

Maura clasps the girl's face in her long-fingered hands and kisses her on both cheeks, clutching her to her bosom like Briar is a beloved child.

"My dearest, Briar," she coos. "I'm glad to see you well. How was your journey?"

Briar casts an uncertain look back at me, looking around for the right words. She eventually settles on;

"Eventful."

Maura chuckles. "I imagine it was."

I clear my throat. The happy reunion is lovely, but I was promised recompense.

Both of their heads swivel my way, wearing matching scowls on their alluring faces.

"You made a bargain with me, LeChance. The piper has come to be paid."

Maura LeChance throws her head back and laughs. The sound curdles my blood. Anything that makes the Fae laugh will be at my expense. I dread her next words.

"You think that's all, little princeling?"

"What's all?"

"Your journey!"

"You said to deliver her to you and so I have."

"I never said delivering her to me was the whole of her journey." She laughs more loudly this time. "The journey is far from over. Briar has a destiny. You'll help her fulfill it."

I grind my teeth together so hard they ache. My fangs throb in time with a pulse that's not there, a phantom sensation. "What fucking destiny?"

Maura flicks her wrist and two chairs slide across the floor, knocking my knees out from under me, and I topple backward into the padded armchair. Briar's chair, of course, stops shy of her legs, so she can sit down comfortably.

"There was prophecy laid down fifteen years ago," Maura begins. "This prophecy foretold ten chosen ones who'd rise up to defeat Morningstar and his great evil."

"What does this have to do with anything," I start.

"Briar is Chosen," Maura interrupts. "She has a part to play. First, to raise the Blue Faerie."

"The Blue Fairie?" Both Briar and I repeat at the same time.

Maura nods. "She was killed not so long ago and her body has been put on display in a House of Oddities in the heart of the City of Secrets. Her body is being constantly mined for pixie dust."

She grimaces at that, as though the very thought is distasteful, then she continues; "The Blue Fairie hid another chosen, Tinkerbell, on a remote island in Neverland." She turns to face Briar. "I know of your power, Briar. I need you to raise the Blue Fairie. We have to find Tinkerbell." Then she turns to me. "Payne will protect you if he wants his chance at becoming human again."

Briar just goggles at her. Good. I'm grateful I'm the only one bewildered as fuck. I knew the world was changing outside the briar wall in the last twenty years, but I hadn't known there'd been a fucking war brewing! Briar seems equally nonplussed. There is only one logical question to ask.

"Who the fuck is Morningstar?"

Maura sags in her chair, as though a leaden cloak has just been draped around her shoulders. Her sigh sounds like the moan of wind through the trees. Disquieting.

"Settle in, children. This is a *very* long story."

SEVEN
BRIAR
Three Days Later

"A war," I whisper, probably for the umpteenth time.

The horror of it is still fresh, though we've been traveling for weeks now. "I can't believe there's been not one but *two* wars while I was asleep."

And not just any sort of war.

A war that threatened to wipe out all of Fantasia. What would have become of me if Morningstar had won? What would have been left of my homeland? Would I have woken to monsters someday, if the magic ever wore off?

Well, I *did* wake to a monster. But he's not half so bad as I once thought. Certainly not in comparison to what we're now facing.

A fully body shiver wracks me and I pull my mother's hunting jacket more tightly about me to ward off the chill. Despite the warmer air outside the cage of briars, I'm cold. I think it has less to do with the mildly chilly spring air

79

and more to do with the two magical links I have attached to me. The first, and most obvious, being Payne. The bond between us feels like a soft silk rope around my throat, as though he could jerk me forward by pulling on it.

The other magical link is with Maura, in the form of ten sapphire and amethyst rings. Each sports a stone the size of my pinkie nail and each is set in a gold or silver band. I keep my hands in my pockets for fear of having them stolen as we pass through city after city. The stones are bespelled and meant to help me control and focus my necromancy. I'll require more instruction from the Blue Faerie and Maura if Payne and I can complete the mission. The rings will supposedly aid me in an effort not to raise dead things on accident.

"I could have been out there *doing* something!" Payne rages. "That Fae bitch could have let us join the Guild and fight off the Great Evil instead of keeping us stuck in that fucking kingdom!"

"Don't talk about Maura that way," I snap reflexively. Even if the curse might have been overkill, I still can't help but come to her defense. "She couldn't have known you wouldn't throw in with the other side." He just glares at me. "Morningstar *and* an army of bloodthirsty vampires holding a grudge? No thanks."

Payne scowls down at his new boots. We've both been given new clothes to wear for the journey, as the clothes we found at the castle were two decades old. I'd kept mother's hunting jacket, but that was about it. We'd both been styled to look far poorer than we were and my hair had been cut to just above my shoulders so I could draw it back into a tail easily or stuff it beneath the cowl, should we be approached.

Maura says that all the Chosen thus far have been female, so Morningstar's forces have been doing literal witch hunts to find the rest of us. It's safer for me to dress as a man.

"Regardless," he mutters. "We ought to have been given a choice!"

"The choice to join Morningstar?"

"No!" he rails at me. "The choice to fight or to remain cursed! We'd have done damn near anything for Maura to lift the curse. Maybe we'd have been able to turn the tide. Maybe this whole prophecy business wouldn't have been necessary."

But... if he'd been made human then, and he'd gone off to fight Morningstar's evil, would I know him now? I doubt it.

The thought bothers me for some reason and I don't try to examine my feelings too closely. Everything's been muddled since I woke. First, to find him kissing me. And then, later, to be bonded so closely to him. And then to hear him speak of his people... He's nothing like the horrid man I've imagined him to be all these years. And he's nothing like the horrid man Maura painted him to be, either. Payne is not an unreasoning, jealous tyrant who slaughtered two lands to slake his lust.

He's... just a lost man, really. Sometimes even more like a boy than a man. He's still youthful and impulsive, as full of piss and vinegar as any man in his early twenties. I wonder if he'll stay that way until the curse is severed. Will he suddenly age twenty years? Will his personality age with his exterior? Will he... change?

I hope not. There's an unexpected tenderness to him when he speaks about his people. A tinge of sadness, too, like looking upon a portrait of a lost love. Sweet and yearning.

It's in those times that I have to resist the urge to climb into his lap and throw my arms around his neck. I know what will follow and I also know it's wrong to want my parents' murderer. Even if he hadn't killed them himself... Even if he'd acted for reasons that seemed right to him at the time… They weren't right. But, even he seems to realize that now. I guess I shouldn't be surprised—he's had twenty years to repent his actions.

At least, that's what I keep telling myself. But, I wonder if I am just imagining his concern or his regret.

Regardless, it's easier to ignore the compulsion to climb onto his lap when he's like this, when bitterness coats every word from his lips and his eyes glow so fiercely red, they rival the last rays of a setting sun.

"Stop brooding," I snap. "Your eyes are glowing! Do you want to get us captured in Nighburrow?"

Payne shakes his head like a dog trying to slough off water. He still looks vexed, but when he glares out at the horizon after, his eyes are indigo, not crimson. He increases his pace, climbing the rest of the steep incline too quickly for me to trail him.

I breathe a small sigh of relief. He's
behaving at least. We're cresting a steep hill
that promises to place us directly above
Nighburrow. Suddenly, Payne staggers, bracing
his hand against a tree. I follow him the rest of
the way up. His eyes have bled to crimson
again, but I can't even chastise him for it. He
looks like he's been struck in the chest, his
hand resting above the place where his heart
ought to beat.

I'm at his side in seconds, placing one hand
on his shoulder to steady him. It feels good to
be touching him, satisfying something deep in
me. The blood bond or something… else?

"What's wrong?"

He drags in several unnecessary breaths.
"Blood."

I check myself surreptitiously. "I'm not
bleeding. Are you hungry? Do you need to
feed?"

I've watched him feed in the other towns
we've passed through. Most often on
prostitutes he pays off afterward. The twist of
jealousy in my chest had ached the entire time
he'd drunk his fill, leaving me with questions
as to why I was even having such a reaction in
the first place. Certainly, I didn't care about

him! I didn't even like him on most days. A very foolish way to feel, indeed. He couldn't exactly feed on me more than once a week. We'd been traveling for almost four now.

Payne shakes his head. "No. It's... It's hard to explain, especially since I've never felt it before. Must be my connection to you manifesting some sort of... magical awareness."

"I still don't understand."

"Blood soaks this ground. There was a battle. Can't you sense the dead?"

Now that he's mentioned it, I can.

I hadn't noticed it upon waking. Every sensation was strange. I'd acted out a pantomime of life for so long, with Maura's help. She taught me speech, the basics of how to use my body, taught me about history and the like. But it wasn't living. Not truly. But now, after waking and actually moving about in the world, I had a sense of deja vu so strong, I wasn't sure exactly what was normal for a human woman to feel.

Slowly, over the course of weeks, I've been able to sort out my magic from everyday sensations. I can feel death. Not just human death, either. I can feel animals, the layers of dead leaves and layers of dead bark on trees.

Death is everywhere. If I'm not seeking it out, it blurs into the background, like the background drone of cicadas.

Now that Payne has mentioned it, I can feel the shapes beneath the ground. He's right. The whole place is saturated with blood. The rotting bodies of many dead are clustered at the edge of Nighburrow, thrown haphazardly into a mass grave. Most of the human bodies are just bone at this point. The inhuman ones have a slightly different energy and rot more slowly. There are a few truly massive shapes that still thrum with enough latent power to be scary.

I rub at the gooseflesh that speckles my arms.

"I feel it," I acknowledge with a nod. "This place has the pall of death hanging over it."

"It must have been a massive battle," he agrees. "It's potent and I imagine I'm only picking this up secondhand. It has to be worse for you." He looks at me then. "Are you alright?"

I glance at him obliquely, studying his face. He's facing the town again, hand still braced on the tree. His face is tilted slightly toward me, tracking me in his periphery, observing me without being obvious about it. He's somber but there is a hint of concern in his eyes. He seems like he means it.

It warms a small, girlish part of me. Aside from Maura, I've never had someone care. Maybe he's looking out for me simply to break the curse. Maybe it's out of sentimentality. But he's truly looking out for me and I can't find it in myself to reject that warmth. I'll need all the warmth and hope I can to weather what's coming. From what Maura tells us, the war with Morningstar is imminent, now that he's escaped his prison.

And I'm a linchpin in this coming conflict, whether I like it or not.

Shaking off the chill, we begin down the sloping hill toward Nighburrow. Maybe it's the magical residue from the bloody battle, but the hill doesn't sport much grass. It's easy to slip and fall in the mud. The town itself looks ramshackle. It's easy to spot the foundations of old houses under many of the bungalow-style homes. Some haven't even been repaired at all, the stone or wood remains jutting from the ground like broken teeth. What sort of cataclysm had befallen the place that they didn't seem to have recovered after fifteen years?

My feet slide out from under me and I yelp, my boots digging muddy trenches for a few feet before I tip backward, toward the unforgiving slope of the hill.

Payne is there in an instant, capturing me in his strong arms, holding me upright, though he slides a little as well, muddying one pant leg up to the knee as he sinks a foot in to slow our descent. He's panting with the effort of anchoring us, but it does slow our descent so we don't slide to the foot of the hill. We do eventually come to a quivering halt at the base of the hill, Payne still holding me.

We stay like that for a moment that seems to stretch for much longer. Our faces are close, his indigo eyes intent on my face. His arms flex a little around me. I can feel the strength in them. He could wring me out like a cloth if he wished. Tear me limb from limb. But, he won't.

My hands have fallen to his waist, resting just above his belt. He has a knife tucked into his belt and other weapons hiding on the rest of him. He doesn't truly need them when he has strength, speed, and deadly, tearing fangs that can rip someone's throat completely from their body.

I stare up at him in that frozen instant, quivering like a leaf in a gale. I'm not afraid of him. I'm more afraid of the aching yearning I feel as he holds me. The bond between us tightens like a crimson thread, of the sort Maura tells me binds souls together.

Fate.

In that moment, I just want him to touch me. Take me down to the muddy ground and kiss me until I'm breathless. Let whatever follows follow and damn the consequences.

Payne leans in with only a trace of hesitance, eyes locking on my mouth, his own lips parting. A soft, eager sound escapes him. It makes my heart leap. Then he leans in, removing those inches separating us so his cool breath fans over my face.

And just before our lips can touch, a loud, obnoxious voice splits the night.

"Oi! You two are trespassing!"

We jerk apart like a sharp, static shock has erupted between us. My heart beats faster, frightened by the new figure who's loping out of the town toward us. A twinge of disappointment makes my heart hurt.

Payne steps away from me, letting his hands drop. Again, disappointment aches so strongly in my chest, I almost cry out.

He turns to face the stranger, stepping a little in front of me, trying to shield me from view. It's a pointless gesture since the man has seen me already. More than that, I've got enough power to draw dead things from the ground and send him running from here to Sweetland if I like. There are many dead things here to choose from, as well. I don't make a move to do anything, because he's not my enemy. At least, he hasn't proven himself as one yet. Regardless, Payne is already advancing.

"Don't kill him!" I hiss at his retreating back, knowing his keen ears will pick up on my words, even if the new man doesn't.

The old man stops shy of the hill and when he's stationary, I can finally see him properly. He looks awful. His skin sags off him, like he might have once been a gourmand but had spent the last eight months in a famine. I can't see any evidence of famine in the land but still, it's the impression I get. His hair is gone, like someone took a bristle brush and scraped it all off. His skin is sallow, his eyes almost entirely eclipsed by shadow, the wrinkles around his jaw and neck drooping so low, they form jowls. There's something a little... frantic in his beady black eyes.

"I wasn't aware this town was private property," Payne says smoothly.

If he's prepared to ignore me and rip the old man's throat out, it doesn't show in his tone. Still, I'm nervous. One thing I can say for Payne is that he's unpredictable. And unpredictable is another word for dangerous.

"Last I traveled here, Nighburrow was open to all," Payne says. "Is Mayor Bente still in charge? We once had an understanding with each other. I could speak with him about this... trespassing misunderstanding. Mister..."

"Otger," the old man says, squinting suspiciously at Payne. "An' I'm not sure what jape you're tryin' to pull, boy. You'd still have been in nappies when Otger was Mayor! What understandin' could you have had with 'im? If ye shit, does he hand ye off to yer mum for changin'?"

Otger laughs, but it sounds forced. Payne looks a little off-footed, remembering too late that anything he knows about Fantasia isn't likely to apply now. Though he should be a man of forty, he doesn't look a day over twenty. That may cause problems for us as we travel.

Clearly, Payne needs to keep his big mouth shut.

"Who's in charge then?" Payne snaps. "I'm sure something can be arranged."

"Lady Thalia arrived here months back and she don't like visitors, but for the merchants that come through."

"Tell her we're merchants then. Once she speaks with me, she'll understand," Payne says.

The old man shakes his head. "Can't let you in. Thalia will kill me."

For some reason, I don't think he's exaggerating the voracity of that claim. I tug urgently at one of Payne's sleeves until he turns just enough to look at me.

"Come on, Pay—" I stumble over his name and turn it into a cough before Otger can catch my slip. "Preston. We'll stop at the next town over."

The City of Secrets is still a long way off.

We'll have to camp in dangerous stretches of wood, but it's nothing we haven't already been doing. I'm capable and I have a vampire guardian. I sleep soundly.

Payne's jaw flexes stubbornly. He turns back to face the old man. "We're stopping here."

I tug even more urgently at his sleeve. I know what he's about to do. It's a terrible idea. Even if he sways Otger, he can't capture the mind of every citizen in Nighburrow.

"It's not worth this," I insist in a hushed but firm tone.

But it's too late.

Payne lunges forward, movements as liquid and deadly as a snake strike and then he has Otger's face squeezed between his hands in the next instant. The man's loose skin overflows Payne's palms, like some fleshy waterfall. He stares up at Payne wide-eyed, the crimson glow of the vampire's gaze reflecting in his own. Payne could easily crush his skull and he knows it. He opens his mouth to scream, but doesn't have a chance to give voice to it before Payne speaks.

"Do you hear me, Otger?"

Otger can barely speak, he's so terrified. Even so, when he does, his voice comes out slurred like a drunk's rather than the petrified squeak I think he wants to give voice to.

"Aye."

Payne gives him a sharp-toothed smile. Otger shivers.

"Good. You're going to take us into town. You will put us up in your house until tomorrow morning, if you have the room. If not, you will take us to the nearest inn. Do you have room for myself and my companion?"

Otger nods, moisture dewing in his dark eyes. "Aye, I do. Me wife she... she passed not long after Thalia's arrival. Of the wasting disease that ripped through the town..."

He trails off, shudders even more violently, squeezes his eyes shut as grief draws soft whimpering sounds from him. Or maybe the whimpers are owing to his fear. Either way, I want to shove Payne out of the way, shout to him that he stop this.

"If there's been a plague, we probably shouldn't enter," I point out, getting a firmer grip on his sleeve. "Come on, Payne. Leave him alone and we'll find a cozy place to camp in the woods."

I figure Otger is so high on the power flowing from Payne's eyes, that it won't matter if I call Payne by his name. He doesn't rebuke me for it, either, so I guess I'm right.

"I want to get you properly fed, bathed, and warm, Briar," he insists. "Aren't you tired of sleeping on the hard ground with nothing but me as a pillow?"

I admit I don't like sleeping on beds of pine needles and rotting remnants of the underbrush. Having him as a pillow... that I don't mind quite as much.

"I just... I just don't want to take any chances," I say as I look at Otger, who is still staring at Payne but now his jaw has gone slack and he's drooling from one side of his mouth. Clearly, he's completely on vampire magic overload.

"Just one night," Payne coaxes, catching sight of my torn expression. "We'll leave at dusk tomorrow and find some miserable place to shelter in next time." He frowns at me. "For tonight, I'd like to sleep in a bed."

"Fine," I relent after another few seconds. "But an inn, please. The poor man looks like he's suffered enough."

Payne releases Otger at last and gives him a push toward town. Otger stumbles and almost doesn't catch himself, sliding in the mud. When he does get his feet under him, he's swaying a little. I've seen Payne use his mesmerism to

feed on men if no prostitutes were available.
They always appeared a little drunk afterward.
And Payne never seems entirely… comfortable
feeding on me. For my own part, I find it quite
funny.

"Lead the way," he says.

Otger nods absently and begins to trek back
in the way he came. Payne is at his side in
moments and I'm left on the hillside, stewing in
a thick sense of foreboding. Something's wrong
here and Payne's too impetuous to notice. I
hope whatever it is won't get us both killed.

"Coming?" he calls back to me jovially.

I sigh. "Do I have a choice?"

"Have you ever?"

And the sad truth is that the answer to that
question is a resounding 'no'.

EIGHT
PAYNE

Otger had shown us to the only inn Nighburrow had to offer. Then he staggered back to his empty home afterward, as I'd instructed him via mesmerism. His will had crumbled like dry cheese beneath my gaze. Which was odd. From a man of his age, I expected a little more struggle. The mind gets set in its ways like a stubborn old oak, not easily bendable when humans reach a certain age. The man had reacted like a young man or perhaps even a man in his prime. No more than thirty.

I'm beginning to wonder if Briar did not have a good point on the hill. There's something... off about this place. Something that has nothing to do with the blood steeped ground or the clear evidence of its earlier destruction. It seems strangely... empty. Even if plague has wiped out most of the citizenry, there should be some sign of the life that once thrived here. Boarded up windows, the smell of putrefaction wafting out into the street, carts piled high with the dead. The sense of... new death that I can pick up from Briar sometimes.

Yet, here there's nothing. The silence seems sinister.

I wonder who this Lady Thalia is that Otger spoke of. Or, more pointedly, *what* she is.

Briar begins stripping out of her clothes the second the door of our room closes. I watch her for a few seconds, lips parted. I'm not sure what I mean to do. Tell her to stop?

"Don't you fucking dare," Tarquis' growl tickles my ear. *"Watch the show, you fool."*

I've gotten very good at ignoring Tarquis. Part of me is inclined to agree with him. The peasant shirt is off and she's struggling with the breeches. I can offer to help her out of them, slide them down her smooth, milky thighs and plant a kiss above her mound. Would she squeal or slap me? She seemed receptive earlier. Maybe I could...

No.

I drop my gaze to the ground instead. Tarquis' snarl becomes louder in my head, cursing a small moral streak I've never been able to completely quash.

"What are you doing?" I demand, now rightly shocked at her lack of concern regarding the fact that she's near naked and I am, after all, only a man.

From my vantage point, I see her breeches hit the floor next and then, oh Gods, her small clothes. If I drag my eyes up her shapely legs, I'll be treated to the sight of her nude. With intense concentration, I force my gaze to the floor. The effort of holding myself in check is physically painful. I'm so hard, it's difficult to think.

"Stripping," she replies curtly. "You should too. We can share the bath and after that, we'll gather some provisions and go."

I'm not sure if I should be more startled at her announcement that we can share a bath or that she wants to leave so soon.

I frown down at the floor. "Leave?" I ask, deciding that subject is safer for the moment.

Briar's shudder rocks all the way to her toes. "There's something very wrong here, Payne. Can't you feel it? Every single person in this town is dying."

"Otger said there was a plague sweeping through..."

"That's not what I'm talking about. It's something… different."

I shrug. "Regardless, I don't think it will affect us."

She frowns up at me. "How can you say that?"

I shrug. "I'm dead and you're linked to me. Thus, we shouldn't be affected by whatever might be killing the citizens here, whether plague or otherwise."

"Look at me, Payne," she says and I swallow hard as I do just that. I don't want to look at her—not while she's currently in her state of undress. I mean, I really want to look at her… but I shouldn't. "I need you to look me in the eyes and know I'm serious."

I almost ignore the command a second after I've given in. I know if I see her this way, I'll never be able to *unsee* it. I'll crave her like blood, like I'd once craved air to breathe. And I'm her enemy. At some point, after the curse is lifted, she'll leave. She can't love the bastard who was responsible for her kingdom's demise. I understand that. I understand vengeance and the many forms it can take.

I look away from her.

"Payne, look at me," she repeats.

Slowly, reluctantly, I unglue my eyes from the floor and look at her. The sight nearly knocks me breathless.

She's made of full, soft curves. The candlelight in the room casts interesting shadows over her body, the flickering light painting the rest of her a soft amber. Her hair seems almost black. It's unbound and hanging near her shoulders now, like a fire-cast shadow around her head. I like it. Her sage eyes almost glow as she watches me drink her in.

"My eyes are up here," she reminds me gently as I fixate on the other, rather appetizing parts of her body. It's an effort to drag my mind out of my pants for long enough to hear anything she's saying.

"What?" I manage to slur rather stupidly.

"I said we need to bathe, grab supplies and go."

"What was the point in coming then?"

"To wash up, to take a few minutes rest. To figure out where we go from here."

"I believe you are overreacting."

She frowns. "The bodies of these people look elderly, but their souls don't match. Almost all of them feel like they're at most thirty or even younger."

"I felt something… similar from Otgar," I admit, though I don't want to.

She nods. "It's like they're aging a year every day or something. Soon enough they'll…"

"Die," I finish for her and she nods. "Is it witchcraft?"

Briar shrugs and the motion does interesting things to her breasts. My mouth feels very dry in that instant. I want a taste of her. I want more than a taste.

"I'm not sure. That seems like something Maura would be able to tell us, if she were here. But, she's not and I don't want to take any chances. We need to get out of here as soon as possible. I'll take you as a pillow over being a witch's plaything, if witchcraft is what's going on here." She pauses, then faces me with a tight jaw. "Now strip."

I untuck my shirt from the breeches with a barely audible sigh. I had been looking forward to a bed and the chance to hold her more firmly against me. I'm fumbling with my belt when Briar approaches me, stilling my fingers and replacing them with her own. She huffs out an impatient breath.

"Faster, Payne."

She yanks the belt through the loops and lets it clatter to the ground before starting on the buttons of the breeches. She pulls them down with equal impatience, though stills when my cock springs free.

"Oh," she says in surprise and then swallows audibly.

I've neglected to wear underthings for days, preferring to walk without them. I'd done it that way for years before her and will probably do so for years after.

Briar's pink top lip touches her lower lip for a second as she stares at it. My cock twitches hard in response.

A breath actually hisses out through my teeth when she cups the base of it gingerly, studying it with a strange curious fascination. I can't tell if she's excited by looking at it or merely inquisitive.

"I've never seen a man's… manhood in person before," she murmurs, almost to herself. "Maura showed me magically induced illusions when she taught me lessons about the differences between men and women's bodies, but…"

Briar's hand strays down further, cupping my balls, rolling them gently. I can't stop a moan from escaping me. It feels too damn good.

She glances shyly up at me. "Do you want me to stop? Does it hurt?"

"Gods, no! To both." I pause for another moment. "But if you keep touching me, I'm going to... something will happen, Briar."

"Something will happen?" she repeats and looks up at me, eyes wide. "What?"

"Something... messy. You ought to release me now if you want to take that bath and quickly raid the larders before we... depart."

A glint of something wicked shines in her eyes. "What will happen if I don't release you?"

I groan again. "If you don't stop that, I'm going to need time to deal with the... problem."

"Problem?"

"You can't bring a man to near completion and then leave him hanging, Briar," I nearly bark. "If such happens, it's not without... pain for the man."

"Are you near completion?"

"Close enough."

"Then complete."

I shake my head. "This isn't how these things are supposed to go."

"I want to watch you complete," she says with headstrong determination.

I groan. "You don't even have the terminology correct, Briar."

"What should I call it?"

"Nothing," I answer and start to pull away from her but she holds my cock even more tightly, like she's unwilling to yield her toy.

She looks up at me, her face full of anticipation. "I'd... I'd like to know what it feels like to have a man inside me."

"You've lost your damned mind!" I say and try to yank my cock away but she's got it tight and, truthfully, I'm not fully committed to pulling away.

"I haven't lost my mind," she barks at me. "I've done nothing in my life, Payne. Walking from Maura's castle to Nighburrow has been the highlight of my life, thus far, which speaks to how sad it's been up to this point. And I wake to discover the nation has nearly been destroyed while I slept and the only thing preventing cataclysm once again is me and a handful of others!"

"Your point?"

She breathes in deeply. "My point is that I want to experience life, Payne. If we are headed into war, there's a good chance I'm going to die before I ever get a chance to live."

"You aren't going to die," I respond immediately, hating the idea. "I won't allow it."

I'm not sure who is more surprised by my words—Briar or me. She breathes in deeply. "It's war and that means you don't know what will happen so you can't say that. Not everyone will survive. Maura says several Chosen Ones have already come close to dying." She looks at my cock again and starts stroking it up and down, as if she's talking to it.

"What does this have to do with me?" I demand, finding it hard to speak because the warmth of her hand feels so good.

"I just want to experience life," she says. "I want to love and be loved. I want to see the world and I want a million other things I'll never get to have."

"Will you stop talking like that? You sound as if you're committing to a death sentence."

"I might be!"

"And you might not be."

She frowns at me. "Regardless, I just want to make love to someone before I die," she whispers. Then she looks up at me again, eyes full of unshed tears. "Why are you trying to talk me out of this?"

"Because…" I start but then lose my stream of thought. "Because… I don't want you to hate me more than you already do."

Her eyebrows furrow in the center of her forehead. "I don't hate you."

"You should."

Most of my ardor has cooled at this sudden and uncharacteristic display of emotion. She's been angry, defiant, crass, teasing, and scared. I've never seen her distraught. It's my fault. I'm the reason she didn't grow up to marry a handsome prince and live a good life before needing to face the Great Evil.

"Well, I don't." She takes a deep breath. "And I still want what I want… to understand what it feels like to be… with a man."

"You don't want that man to be me," I say quietly.

"You don't know what I want!"

I shake my head. "Briar, I'm no good."

"You're the only person I want."

"I'm the only man you know."

She glares at me. "Make love to me, Payne. I want to know what it's like."

It's hard to argue with her when she's staring up at me like this. I know we should be moving on. If she's right and there's magic here, that means we're in danger. But... fuck it all. I can't look away from her and I can't stop thinking about… I can't stop thinking about what she's asking of me. She deserves to know what it's like between a man and a woman. I can understand her interest, of course. And after all I've robbed from her already, can I truly be cruel enough to purloin the only chance she's likely to get (well, anytime soon, anyway) to feel a man?

Or, am I just thinking this way out of my own selfish want and need? I guess it's impossible to know for sure.

"Please, Payne," she whispers.

"Fuck," I grumble.

Slowly, without breaking eye contact, I kick my boots off and peel the breeches from my body, tossing them to join the pile of her clothes. It leaves us both bare, both staring very intently at each other. It seems wrong for her to be kneeling at my feet. She's a princess. And she's Chosen. I'm prince of nothing and no one.

I reach down and clasp her arms, raising her to her feet, bringing her flush to my body. There's a space of a few breaths where we continue to stare at one another. Then she stands on tiptoe, pressing her mouth very gently to mine.

The kiss is sweet. Almost painfully chaste. Her lips are cool and I'm beginning to think she won't warm much beyond the temperature around her. Not without serious effort, anyway. The kiss becomes less innocent moments later, when she slides her hands around my neck and hauls me down to her, using her leverage to angle the kiss in her favor. The slick sweetness of her tongue skims across my lips and I moan, surrendering to her will.

She presses us both back, toppling me onto the bed like I'm the maiden and she the dastardly villain here to take my virtue, and not the other way around. She presses herself to me, a soft and welcome weight on my chest, straddling my waist eagerly. She moves from my mouth quickly, trailing sharp bites down my throat in a move so erotic, I almost climax. No other woman has ever bitten me.

I'm so overcome by the feel, taste, smell of her, that it takes me a second to realize she's reaching between us for my cock again, shimmying down so she can position herself above it.

"Briar, don't," I groan. "It will hurt. Let me..."

She silences me with a look. Her eyes shine luminescent green. "Maura says it's uncomfortable no matter which way it's done. This is my choice, Payne. Please. Let me do this the way I want."

I hesitate a moment longer, loathe to hurt her more, but unable to think clearly with her hand slowly teasing my cock until I'm breathless. Her hands fumble just a little, nerves plain in the way she moves. If I were a good man, I'd ease her off me, soothe her until she falls asleep and guard the door in case of attack. But I'm not a good man and I fear rejecting her now will make her hate me in earnest.

But, I won't let her lose her maidenhead like this. "Let me satisfy you," I start but she's already guiding me to her entrance.

"Briar," I start but then I can't speak as I feel her slowly ease the tip of me inside. Just the mere sensation of her sinking onto me makes my back arch, sliding my cock in a little further. She's incredibly tight and the feel of her is pure, pleasurable torment.

She settles herself onto me, not pausing until I'm seated fully inside. She yelps slightly at the feel of my head busting through her virgin flesh but then she takes a deep breath and the slight expression of pain on her face is gone. She shivers, the motion making her full breasts move in enticing ways. Her nipples are a light pink, like a pale summer rose. I slide my hands up her body to cup them, to pluck at them until she lets out a soft cry of pleasure.

When she begins to move, I'm sure I'll lose it right then and there. She goes slow at first, but gains speed quickly, her breath coming in soft little gasps on every down stroke. I want to grab her and hold her in place while I push up into her and pull out again but I stop myself. I want her to take her pleasure from me—to go at her own speed… to ride me as she likes. Pleasure quickly replaces any discomfort on her face as she gets her rhythm, her core playing my cock like a flute. She moves faster and faster still, raking her nails down my chest, drawing blood. I don't care. The scent of it just adds another layer of pleasure to the act. Even if it's my own.

She's shining with candlelight and power, all shadows and pale planes. She's death and blood and ecstasy rolled into one irresistible package. Maura LeChance knew what she was doing when she sent me to find Briar. She had to know I'd be helpless in the face of this tempestuous woman. Willing to give my all. Anything she wants. It was probably Maura's idea of a punishment, dragging me still lower to grovel like a dog at Briar's feet.

But this is not an unkind master and Briar is someone I can gladly bow to. So I drive into her when she urges, roll her beneath me at last and explore every inch of skin I can reach with my lips. And when my teeth sink into the swell of one breast, I have to muffle her scream of pleasure. She shakes beneath me and I feel my own orgasm busting through.

I shove my length as far into her as I can and feel myself filling her with my seed. It takes me a moment to calm down and come back down from the exquisite high.

It has been so long. So long since I've been inside a woman. And yet, I can't help but wonder why this feels different. Maybe it's been too long since I had sex, but there's something between us… it could be the bond that's making me feel so close to her. I can't be sure. I just… I just want to hold her.

When I roll to one side of her, I pull her in close so I can press her body to mine. She's sheened in sweat, but I don't care. For this moment, at least, she's mine. I don't want to let go.

Of course, that's when a horrendous sound splits the night air and our door topples inward, hitting the hardwood floor with force enough to split some of the boards.

In the gap stands a woman so beautiful and so utterly inhuman it is terrifying. No human woman's skin glows like she was sculpted from emerald. No human woman has hair with the color and texture of spider's thread. And no human woman I've ever met has eyes the color of onyx, with just as much warmth to them.

She's carrying a struggling Otger by the loose skin at the back of his neck. I just stare at him. He looks even worse than he did before. The skin is drawn taut across bone, liver spots like huge brown ink stains take up most of his skin. He looks like a stooped, decrepit old man. And as I watch, the impossible woman (Fae perhaps, it's too hard to tell) turns him and plants a firm kiss on his mouth, muffling the piteous whine that's been easing from between his yellowed teeth.

Every hair on my neck stands on end at what happens next.

What was left of Otger simply... dissolves. The skin tightens still further on the bones, the eyes just evaporate right out of their sockets like droplets of water on a summer day. When she drops him, he is just leathery flesh and a pile of bones. He rattles audibly to the floor, mouth hanging wide, black eye sockets unseeing.

Briar screams and I feel my own mouth drop open at the horrible sight.

The woman smiles pleasantly at us, though the expression never reaches those flinty eyes.

"Ah, the trespassers. Good of you to stay put. I do hate chasing down Lady Vita's next meal. So tiresome."

Vita.

The name strikes a chord. One of Morningstar's generals. One of the monsters unleashed by Bacchus' revelry not so long ago. One of Briar's enemies. And one of Vita's attendants has just downed the remaining life force of a man as if she were sipping a draft of ale. There's no way I can fight her without weapons. There's only one thing to do.

"Briar, run!"

NINE
BRIAR

Payne is on his feet in an instant, his hands seizing me by the biceps so hard, it hurts. He drags us to the only exit left to us—the window. When we reach it, he's whipped me around and into a bridal carry before I can so much as cry out. Neither one of us is wearing a stitch of clothing, my body still aches pleasantly from his attentions, and I'm exhausted. It seems strange that fucking should be so exhausting.

We ought to have saved our energies, it seems.

Payne's bare foot strikes the window with such force, the glass shatters outward like a spray of sea foam to a shoreline. It tinkles onto the ground below seconds later. Dozens of jagged shards remain on the sill and I shriek when Payne vaults onto it, cutting himself to ribbons in the process. Blood sluices down the wall to puddle on the floor. I cry his name, but it's too late.

He leaps the three stories to the ground below, dodging a violently green blast of energy coming from Vita's attendant by a mere fraction. I can feel the blistering heat of it and, above us, the air begins to ripple. The wind screams in my ears as we hurtle down to the ground. It takes mere seconds, but feels infinitely longer. My heart lurches and fresh tears squeeze from my eyes when Payne lets out an agonized sound as glass crunches beneath his bare feet.

"You're hurt!" I breathe. "Put me down!"

Payne grits his teeth and begins a loping run toward the other end of town. "We don't have time!"

He holds me even tighter and starts forward. "Where are you going?" I insist, because this isn't the way we came in.

"This way is faster. We'll lose momentum going up the hill."

This way was also more dangerous. More bone-thin shapes emerge from the homes all around us. The occupants only appear alive in the technical sense. All of them are dying, aged to death in a matter of hours or days as the witch sucks the life from them. They're all as brittle as eggshells, but it doesn't matter. If enough of them can hem us in, it won't matter that we're stronger. We'll be outnumbered. Thalia will catch up to us and that will be the end of Briar Rose and Prince Payne.

But how do I stop that from happening? The only weapons we had on our persons were hidden in Payne's belt or various articles of clothing. A belt and clothing that are still in the room at the inn. The only thing I'm wearing at the moment are the rings Maura gifted me before our departure.

And then an idea kindles to brilliant life in my mind.

"Up!" I shout over the cries of the growing crowd of skeleton-like townspeople.

"What?"

"Up," I repeat, jerking my finger upwards for emphasis. "Onto the rooftops. We can reach the outskirts of town faster."

"All that's on the other side is a river, Briar. And I'm not sure if we have time to wade across it."

"Do you trust me?" I glance down as I ask the question, studying his expression. I need him to trust me, now more than ever. I know what I'm asking him to do will make the difference between life and death.

He glances up just long enough to meet my gaze before nodding slowly. "Strangely enough, I do."

I give him a fierce little smile before he leaps, using a stile to go almost ten feet vertically so that we hover above a tiled rooftop very briefly. I yelp a little in fright when we descend, especially when he stumbles just a step, threatening to send us both careening off the roof. He gets his legs beneath him at last, and then we're sprinting.

Nighburrow is almost completely uniform in its height. The houses were grand once and retain a little of their former austerity, if not in style than in height. Each leap could be life-threatening for an average mortal. Not for Payne. Even when he stumbles, takes still more skin off his knees or shins, he gets up, never once letting go of me. I'm growing more and more concerned about his pallor and the blood loss causing it.

Is it safe for me to feed him when we're clear of this place? I wonder.

Perhaps the better question is *will* we get clear of the place?

Almost as if my thoughts summon her, Thalia leaps onto a rooftop one row over from

119

ours. She's nimble as a cat and as poisonous as verdant and deadly as an arrow frog. She thrusts out a hand toward Payne and a stream of green fire, no broader than a silk thread, shoots toward him. Another stream of green fire emerges from another finger, then yet more. She doesn't seem to be perturbed when Payne leaps over the shots directed at him. They crisscross, almost forming a net... no... a web. Then she very calmly steps off her rooftop and onto one of the shining threads.

It holds her weight without effort. She smiles wickedly when she catches sight of my horrified expression and then begins to sprint across what was formerly open air, over the heads of the pitiful mass of humans below, straight towards us. She shouldn't be able to gather speed on that tiny thread of energy and yet...

"Fuck!" Payne hisses when he cranes his neck to look at her.

She'll be on us in minutes, if not less. Payne is fast, but he can't run in midair.

"Jump," I direct, breathless with terror.

"There's nothing down there but..."

"I know. Just jump, Payne."

"Briar..."

"Just get me to the depression beneath the pair of elm trees. I can't explain why."

The patch I'm seeking is just up ahead, nestled between two elm trees. Or what used to be two massive elms. They're nothing but trunks now, big and blocky and carved with the names of the dead that exist in this large, untended grave. Despite the intervening years, grass hasn't spread over the mound of earth atop it. It looks as if it's fresh dug, the magic of whatever's buried beneath keeping it that way.

Payne leaps off the roof just as another blast of super heated air rushes over our heads. I'm absolutely certain it would have boiled skin off bone. He lands wrong and loses his grip on me. I fall and hit the ground hard, pain lancing up my right side as I impact the earth. Digging my nails into the mud, I claw my way forward, rather than trying to recover my feet. I'm too close to give up now.

When I reach the turned earth, I dig my fingers in deep, all the way up to the knuckles, where Maura's rings gleam silver and violet in the moonlight.

"Come to me," I breathe, willing all the panic, the helplessness, the rage I can muster into the call, just as I had when raising my family in the great hall.

I reach down and feel the dead. There are many of them. So many. Plenty for an army but I'm exhausted and hurting, and that means I won't be able to command them for long. So, I reach for the four largest shapes I can feel. When my magic brushes them, I find only two are intact enough. The other bodies are too mangled to raise. Too many pieces missing. Like heads, for one.

My power finds the two large shapes, trickles into them like a stream of cool water, and they began to stir. Then, slowly, they lift their enormous heads and scythe the ground with their claws.

Thalia lands with a thump feet away, smiling like a Cheshire cat as she raises her hands.

"It's time to die, interlopers."

She readies a blast.

And that's when two, enormous dirt-caked dragons burst from the earth and take to the air. Scraps of cloth flutter off them as they do so. It's hard to tell between the darkness and the slick mud that clings to them, but one appears to be bronze and the other a vivid sapphire.

They circle once overhead before the bronze dragon whips around, opening its enormous mouth.

It gets Thalia in its sights and then rains fire down on her head, razing her to ash.

TEN
NOUILLE

The void is peaceful. That's why Veseo hates it so much.

Though largely opposite in temperament and ideals, in this, he and Malvolo are very much alike. Both abhor boredom. Mal liked to fill his hours with whoring and gambling until we met Peregrine…

Regardless, Veseo can't understand why we've been stuck in this half-world. He wants to find Feudejoie, the final resting place for dragon warriors. Family will surely be waiting for us there.

But no Shepherd has come to take us from this middle-world to our rightful resting place. Time means little here. Perhaps we've been dead for mere days. Perhaps it has been far longer. But, we both agree that a Shepherd ought to have tended to our souls by now.

We are not alone here.

Many humans and shifters swim below in the inky water or float in the space between the water and the starry sky. I tend to hover somewhere near the northern star, liking its light the best.

"Where the fuck are they?" Veseo growls, glaring balefully at the blackness all around us. *"We deserve rest!"*

When he rages like this, he sounds like Malvolo. I don't like it. In life, he was such a happy man. Of the seven of us, Veseo and Malvolo are the only ones who favor each other in human form. Veseo with hair such a dark auburn, it almost looks black in the right light. His eyes are dark with the edge of flame at their center. Golden flame, instead of the ember-orange of Malvolo's eyes.

I open my mouth to placate him as I've done many times before, when something in the blackness... stirs. Our surroundings fade little by little, so the void seems less real. I've heard accounts from those claiming to come back from death, drawn toward second life by a regretful Shepherd. It's against the rules, but it has happened.

Those accounts described warmth. Safety and calm.

None of which I feel.

Cold rakes vicious claws through my body, shearing the rest of the illusion away. I suck in a breath and choke on particles of dirt. I try to lift my head and breath the crisp air, but there's only more earth in the way. Worse, something is binding my wings to my body. I begin to panic when I realize what's happened.

I've been buried alive!

My body has been respectfully wrapped in a guild flag or tapestry and laid to rest. But how could someone be ignorant that I still live?

With little other choice, I scythe through the earth, desperately trying to reach the surface, before I truly choke to death on the earth seeping in all around me. One of my thrashing limbs strikes Veseo. Gods, how had they missed the two of us? Is this why we've been trapped in the middle lands? Because we're not truly dead?

I break the surface of the earth with difficulty, sucking in a great lungful of air, coughing out what I've managed to breathe in. Veseo follows soon after, pushing his wings free, taking to the air with one powerful stroke. I do the same moments later, launching my body into the air, riled as I've never been before.

The dirt flies off me and I feel a sense of freedom I haven't felt in far too long.

But there's something... wrong. Something I can't place my finger on. It's like there's a... a tie around my neck, though the burial shroud has come loose and pooled on the ground far below. I examine it curiously, try to follow the ephemeral sensation back to its source. It's magic, undoubtedly. Reve could tell me what sort. He's always been the expert on such things. Not a ruby or gold cent to be found in his horde. Books and maps, and secrets are what he treasures.

I find the wielder of this intense magic lying on the ground and I'm caught off guard.

It's a woman. A very nude, incredibly beautiful woman.

I soar down, to get a better look at her. I almost suspect her to be Belle Tenebris, but for a few things. First, this woman is taller and has almost no curl to her chestnut locks. Belle's hair is far closer to honey or caramel. Belle's eyes are brown, where this woman's are dark green. She has a more... ample chest than Belle.

But Gods is she powerful. Her power leaks into the air around her, bringing the temperature down by degrees. For a moment, it's really all I can do not to land and kneel before her. Part of me yearns toward her with a longing I don't understand. A longing I've never felt before, not even with Peregrine.

Veseo wheels about, eyes narrowing on the shape across from the woman who has freed us from our earthly prison.

Thalia.

One of Vita's favorite handmaidens and one of the more viscous. The war must still be waging if Thalia has cornered this little witchling and her companion, who is standing between Thalia and the girl. Brave of him. Foolish, but brave.

Veseo lets out a brassy cry of defiance and the sound jerks Thalia's attention to our position, almost a mile up. She has only enough time to spot us, to open her mouth in a cry of horror, before a gout of flame as long as a dragon's tail issues from Veseo's mouth, charring the sorceress to cinders. It's not a quick or easy death. She has time to make agonized sounds as the flesh melts off her bones and the heat warps and twists what remains of her skeleton.

The foolish man who stood between the witchling and Thalia seizes the girl around the waist, in a move too swift to be human, leaping adroitly back from the barrage of flame. I eye him with growing dislike. There's something wrong about his aura. He's faster than a mortal and probably stronger too. Pale. An aviary shifter? Perhaps an owl? No.... his eyes are indigo, not amber. I don't want him near the witchling.

I consider pelting him with flame. It's unlike me to be so violent upon waking. In life, I tended to be the universal peacemaker when we lived in the mountains. Malvolo and Veseo fought the most ardently, but Mal had just as many scuffles with Herrick, Maug, and Choro. Only Reve and I tended to stay out of things. So why do I hate this man on sight?

Without consulting with each other, Veseo and I scan the area for more threats, finding only a confused horde of elderly humans milling about on the main road through Nighburrow. Speaking of… the town has been rebuilt. When did that happen? If the war has been waging while we were trapped underground, how would anyone have had the time to rebuild this city which was decimated? As I glance around myself, I realize the buildings seem weathered with age. Impossible.

I'm still bewildered when I land six feet from the witchling and begin to shift to my human form. After so long underground, it's uncomfortable to pare myself down to the smaller shape, like stretching sore muscles. Maybe that's why it takes so long for me to do so. Longer than I remember it ever taking. Behind me, I can hear Veseo doing the same.

The witchling stares at us both in open wonderment as we come to our feet. With some amusement, I see her scan both of us from head to toe, unable to keep her gaze from one part of our anatomies in particular. Human women are usually impressed by the length and girth of shifter men. And dragon shifters are the leaders of the pack, for reasons quite obvious.

I fight not to preen.

"You're dragons..." the woman says, more to herself than either of us. "I had no idea."

She doesn't seem in the least bit concerned that she's naked. That we all are naked. Instead, she stands there, completely brazenly. And I immediately decide I like her. She is a courageous, little thing. No fear.

"No idea about what?" Veseo demands. He's at my side, bristling with energy. I've seen him like this before. If something spooks him, he likes to fight or fuck the fear away. Waking underground and faced with Vita's general certainly qualifies.

"That it was dragons down there, beneath the earth," she says in a very small voice.

"If you didn't know what we were, why did you summon us?" Veseo demands, and even though I can see him fighting to keep his eyes on hers, he falters a few times and his gaze drops to her perfect breasts.

"I needed help and you two were the only ones who weren't rotted or in pieces." She takes a breath. "But, I never imagined you'd be... dragons."

Oh Gods. We *were* dead. No one buried us alive. This witchling called us from the grave! She's no witchling at all—she's a necromancer.

Born of death, swathed in blood, a rose in briar thorns, will lead a cursed legion to counter life's callous scorn.

She's fucking Chosen!

And now I understand why I recognize her. She's almost a perfect copy of Lelita Rose. Which means this girl must be the only survivor of the slaughter.

Briar Rose.

She's the princess Rose.

131

The truth has me reeling.

This girl has to be at least twenty, if not older. She'd been put in eternal sleep five years before the war started, so she'd have been a small girl when we passed on. And that means...

Veseo and I have been waiting in a void for *fifteen years!* The war has been raging on without us. How many of my brothers are in the mass grave we crawled from? I knew Maug and Choro were injured when I breathed my last. Have all of Veles' line passed on? Are Herrick, Malvolo, and Reve in the dirt, as well? A pained sound escapes me.

"My brothers," I say but then lose my voice.

Princess Rose reads the horror playing out on my face and tears well in her eyes. The regret pours off her in palpable waves.

"I'm so sorry," she whispers. "I shouldn't have... I can put you back."

Veseo makes a sound, as well, but it's more like he's swallowed a whoop or a laugh. He lopes forward, stride long-legged and sure. Briar lets out a squeak of surprise when he catches her around the waist, lifts her so her feet dangle off the ground, and spins her like she weighs nothing at all. When he finally sets her on her feet again, he tugs her in close, shoves one hand into her hair, and kisses her with enough passion to scorch the ground around them.

She moans into his mouth. Veseo's kisses are like that, or so I've been told. Part of his magic, I think. Infectious joy. Peregrine loved him best for that reason. He laughs often, loves deeply, and doesn't hold grudges for long. And apparently he's a skilled lover, though I don't have cause to know. We never shared Peregrine at the same time.

"Don't you dare put us back, witchling," he says as he smiles down at her.

Before I can take another breath, Briar's would-be knight lunges forward with a growl, shoving Veseo away from the witchling with enough force to make Veseo stumble. He has a huntsman's strength or better, but it's not until his eyes flash a vivid crimson and his lips pull back from his teeth that I know him for what he truly is.

Vampire.

This must be the infamous Prince Payne. But... how can that be possible? Yet, all signs point to this being exactly that man. So, why

133

does Princess Rose travel with her family's murderer?

"Keep your hands off her, you fucking reptile," he snarls, looking first at Veseo and then at me. "Or I'll make you a dead man all over again."

Veseo's eyes flash copper, the energy of his beast rising once more as he anticipates a challenge. He's not prone to violence either, except to protect a female. Then does he believe he's… protecting this one? Against Payne?

Is it her magic that makes us respond this way to her? I can't tell.

Briar Rose looks dazed as Veseo lets out another pealing laugh.

"Fuck, it's good to be alive again!" He throws a playful smile over his shoulder at me. I haven't moved from the spot, still rooted with worry for my brothers. Apparently Veseo has forgotten about them in his celebration of his own life.

"Come, Nouille," he says. "Don't be bashful. You ought to thank the witchling for her service."

"She's a necromancer," I say.

"And don't think to fucking touch her," Payne says as he takes a step towards me. He looks at Veseo again. "Either of you."

Briar thrusts her comparatively small body between them, soft hands braced against each of their chests.

"No! Don't fight! We don't have time for any of this. Someone probably saw what happened and is running to tell Vita even now. We can't stay here!"

Vita's name cuts through both men's anger like a dagger through fresh-churned butter. Payne grimaces, but takes a step back from her, and Veseo does the same. Both men are glowering at each other, like they'd like nothing better than to tear each other's throats out.

"What would you like us to do, Mistress?" Veseo says finally.

Spots of color appear in her waxy cheeks. "I'm no one's mistress, Mr...?"

"Veseo, of the Southern Dragon Clan," my brother says, jutting out his chin proudly. "And the indecisive one behind me is Nouille. And you *are* our mistress. So long as you keep us... alive, so to speak, you control us."

"I don't… I don't understand," she says nervously.

"It means we are yours," Veseo says. "Anything you desire of us, we'll give. We don't have much say in the matter."

"Why not?" she asks.

"Because you called us from the dead," Veseo answers with a shrug.

The color disappears from her cheeks, her eyes flying wide with horror. "You're slaves? I've… I've turned you into my slaves?" Her mouth hangs open in shock and shame. Then she shakes her head. "I can't be responsible for taking your choice away! That wasn't my intention at all!"

I clear my throat and speak for the first time since landing. It's hard to find my voice around her.

"We should rather serve you than remain trapped in the void, Princess Rose," I say. "We're no better off if you lay us to rest. At least now we can help in the war effort." I scuff my bare foot on the ground, hesitant to make the request. Will it sound too bold? "I only ask that we be allowed to find our brothers, if they're still living."

"Of… of course," she says.

136

I don't pull my eyes away from her. "How many were in the grave with us?"

"There were four of you," she says, hands twisting at the hem of her shirt, shamefaced. "I tried to reach the other two... but there were too many... I don't know how to say it."

"Just do," I reassure her.

"I couldn't raise them because... they were in... too many... pieces."

She hesitates over the last word. My heart breaks. It has to be Choro and Maug. Or... maybe Malvolo. I saw him go down, one wing twisted off by Morningstar, like the bastard was picking apart a fly.

But that still means at least three of my brothers are likely still living.

"Of course we can find your brothers," Briar continues. "But Payne and I must reach the City of Secrets first. We need to find the Blue Faerie. She's the only one who can tell us where to find Tinkerbell. And once we do that, it will bring the number of Chosen up to six. We'll be that much closer to defeating Morningstar."

I blink and exchange a look with my brother. Six Chosen? Fuck me. We've missed a great deal. There's really only one thing we can say, and the answer isn't even compelled out of us.

"We're coming with you," Veseo says.

"No fucking way," Payne responds.

But we both ignore him. This isn't his choice to make.

"You gave us life," I say to the princess. "Let us safeguard yours."

"I was safeguarding her life just fine," Payne argues, glaring at each of us in turn.

She looks at him and smiles, putting her hand on his chest and the gesture seems to instantly calm him. "Payne… we must think about this rationally."

She pulls her lip between her teeth and the gesture is so enticing, I feel myself growing hard. She notices and fresh color floods her face. I hide a smile. It's nice to be noticed.

"Alright," she says finally.

"Bloody fuck," Payne grumbles, shaking his head.

"But just one thing," the princess continues.

"Name it," I say.

She stares at my manhood like it's something dangerous that might come after her at any moment.

"Put on some… pants, please. You're going to hurt someone with those monsters," she finishes with a little laugh.

Veseo smirks. "Anything to please my mistress. I don or remove my pants at your pleasure."

"You'll keep your fucking pants on," Payne says, grumbling something else I can't make out.

"As soon as we find some," I say and make a point to motion to the fact that he's not wearing a stitch of clothing, either.

Then I turn back to face the princess. Her blush is so red now, I can practically feel the heat coming off her.

"We will find clothing as our first line of business," she says.

I smile at her. "Yes, mistress."

ELEVEN
VESEO

If I had any choice in the matter, I'd kill the vampire where he stands.

The prince is a peacock, constantly preening in front of Mistress Briar. Full of the swaggering arrogance that comes from noble birth. Worse, it's clear she's besotted by him. Any chance they have, they're fucking. Sometimes near enough to the camp so we can hear. And I am quite certain Prince Dickhead does so on purpose. He wants us to know he's claimed her.

I can only grind my teeth impotently as I hear her moans echo through the trees. I spend my nights plotting ways to get her alone. She wants me, I know that. I can feel the pull through the bonds of her magic. I still remember the way she moaned against my lips when I kissed her. I only wish she'd do so with me between her thighs.

I catch Nouille staring at her too, with a sort of sweet longing that breaks my heart. Nouille, the gentle giant of the Southern Dragon Clan. In the past, he tended to fade into the background, dwarfed by the much stronger personalities of our other brothers. Malvolo, the malcontent. Herrick, with steady wisdom and renowned healing ability. Reve, the magician. Maug, the fearsome berserker. Choro, the jester of the family.

No one payed attention to the peaceful, loving Nouille. And, even now, I feel him taking up his familiar position in the shadows, in the background of the four of us.

Nouille's a good fighter, but no more than any of us. He doesn't like fighting, never has. Some consider him weak, devalue the peace he can bring to a situation. No one values peace until it's gone.

My brother and I are currently pacing a few yards back, watching the sway of Briar's shapely hips as we approach the City of Secrets. She's walking hand in hand with Payne, their fingers intertwined.

"I don't understand what she sees in the pompous git either," I say at regular volume. I know the vampire will hear me and Briar won't. Which is just as well, because my comment is meant for his ears.

Nouille sighs. "Don't pick a fight with Payne. We can't afford to enter the city injured with Morningstar's Generals on the prowl again."

All seven of them.

I shudder to think how Fantasia fares now that Morningstar is back. They are ill-equipped for war, counting on magical seals to keep the Great Evil contained for another decade or more. As if Morningstar and his ilk could ever be contained by such a flimsy spell.

Trust humans to become complacent when the threat is out of sight.

I lower my voice so that only Nouille can hear my next words. Payne won't react well to them, the selfish prick. "If you want her, ask. I won't stand in your way."

Nouille glances up from his study and contemplation of Briar's backside. "She…" he starts.

"Wants us both. You've felt it through our bond as much as I have."

He nods and then looks at me. "Payne is against it."

"And who the fuck cares?" I demand. "She's a princess and she's the one who makes

142

the decision as to what… or *who* she wants, as far as I'm concerned."

Noille nods and grows silent for a few seconds. "I know you want her too, Veseo."

'Want' isn't the right word. It's likely the magic, but I feel for her what I once felt for Peregrine. The desire to take a mate. Truthfully, it could never have worked between Peregrine and me. Two different beast forms would have clashed and likely killed any children we had. But with Briar... she's human. Dragons breed with humans well enough.

"We could share her, like we did with Peregrine," I offer. "If she wants that, of course."

"You wouldn't mind sharing her?"

"I was never the selfish one, Nouille. That was Maug. I share well enough. I want you to be happy, whether we love a woman together or separately. Besides, we are bonded to her now, so what choice do we have? We will always feel this… connection to her, this need for her."

"Yes," Nouille says and nods as he drops his attention to the ground. Then he looks at me again. "What of the vampire?"

"As I said before, whatever the princess wants, the princess gets. And if the vampire can't handle it or doesn't want to, he can find the door."

He smiles gently and returns his gaze to Briar. "It's not a half bad idea, Veseo."

***

It happens near dusk, as we're readying for supper and then bed. Fate has been kind enough to provide a roof over our heads, at last. The home is old, clearly abandoned, and a shell of its former self. It lists hard to one side, the roof buckling beneath the elements. Still, the front room is intact and the hearth is usable. I'm preparing the fare Payne caught for supper. Nouille has stretched out on the floor, basking in the warmth of the fire. Payne has curled in the opposite corner, with Briar in his lap.

I can't help the flash of envy I feel upon seeing them.

Just twenty miles to go and we'll reach the City of Secrets. We could make the journey tonight if we pressed. If one of us carried Briar in our arms, we could use our full speed. We've adopted a rather gimpy pace in order to allow

144

Briar to keep her pride. She already feels like the weak link in our not-so-merry band of misfits. She's wrong, of course. She's anything but weak. Truth be told, I've never seen powers like hers. She's destined for greatness. Well, of course she is—she's Chosen, after all.

Nouille and I have grown progressively weaker as the days go by, so much so that I've begun to worry we've contracted something and are growing ill. What diseases to the dead get? Some sort of necrotic plague that rots one from the inside out? I can't see any sores or feel maggots wriggling in my belly, but it doesn't mean they're not there.

Payne and Briar are whispering conspiratorially to each other. I can tell already they're going to slip off to fuck before supper. He's nuzzling her neck, placing kisses along the pale column of her throat, drawing gasps from her when the edge of his fangs skim her skin. I'm midway through roasting a hare on a spit when my body goes entirely limp, the muscles slackening with alarming speed. My legs go out beneath me and it's all I can do not to fall in the fire.

"Veseo!" Briar screams at the same time Nouille turns to face me.

The world spins rapidly like a top, the muted colors of the night streaking together in shades of black, gray, and navy. My head strikes a rock on the way down, but I barely feel the pain of it. I can make out the muffled thump when Nouille hits the ground moments later.

Briar scrambles from Payne's lap with a cry of alarm, running toward us. Before she can reach us, however, the world goes black.

I don't know how long I'm out but I come to with a heavy weight pressing onto my chest, crushing the air from my lungs.

I die without even getting a glimpse of her face.

TWELVE
BRIAR

"No, no, no, no!"

My protests streak together until they're almost one word. I scramble forward, unsure of which body I should kneel over first. Veseo and Nouille stare sightlessly up at the night sky, pupils rapidly dilating, their skin going waxy and gray before my eyes. They appear to be… very certainly… dead.

Moments ago, they'd been acting normal, Veseo casting a sullen glare at Payne. Neither man likes the other much. Nouille has grown on Payne and, if I'm honest, he's grown on me. He's sweet, a gentle giant who handles everything with care, even me. He carries my things without complaint and when I catch him staring at me, my heart almost melts. The honest, almost puppyish devotion is endearing. Hs features are soft and he speaks softly. I want to climb into his lap and kiss him until he smiles. I believe I know the type of man he is— he'd make love to me, not fuck me. And the

147

thought of finding out if my guesses are true causes flashes of excitement to stir through me.

But, now he's gone. There's no spark in him.

No!

It had felt like the snap of rope pulled past its limits. For days now, something has strained inside me, pulling like a tendon worked too hard. And when it broke, both men collapsed... much as I'd done—before Payne bonded me to him.

I can't help but wonder if that's less of a coincidence that maybe it appears to be.

Though the panic doesn't recede, the thought at least gives me an idea of what's happening.

My power isn't strong enough without training. I could barely keep myself animate before the bond with Payne. He's become the anchor I need to keep myself alive. Veseo and Nouille need an anchor, too.

"Payne," I say urgently, waving him over. My voice is choked with emotion. I don't want to cry. My tears won't help Nouille or Veseo. But Payne can help them. I just hope he will. I look over at him when he appears beside me. "I need your help."

He moves until he's kneeling by Veseo, studying the unconscious man with disinterest. When he eyes Nouille, something that appears to be concern washes over his expression for a second or so. Then it's gone. It's good to know my men don't *entirely* hate each other.

I pause. When had I started to think of them as *my* men?

"What's wrong with them?" he asks, waving a hand uselessly over Veseo's face as though it might wake him. Veseo's expression doesn't twitch with annoyance, like it might in life.

"My power," I explain, throat too tight to allow for an elaborate answer. "It's not enough that I brought them back to life and that my will animates them now," I say, wondering if my words make sense. I turn to face Payne. "I need you to do the same for them... as what you did for me."

His eyes lock with mine, the indigo shade growing just a little colder.

"You know what it will do, Briar," he says quietly. "My blood interacting with your power, with them..."

His blood and my power bind us together. And we can't resist one another. The tie

149

between us is whole—irrevocable and wholly binding. No matter how hard I might try to fight it, the bond will always win. I can't get enough of him. And that means… If we all bond together... it's like a marriage. Each of us loving the other. Wanting each other. We'll have to share one another always. The bond is permanent. Well, as far as I can tell. And Payne seems to believe it, as well.

Regardless, I can't just let them die. Not again.

"Please," is all I can manage to say through the rising tide of grief. I've raised them, spoken to them, known them. Losing them now feels like amputating a limb and burning the stump. It's too great a loss to bear when it can be undone.

"I don't know what this could mean, Briar," he starts. "I've never been bonded to a man. I've never even heard of it ever being done."

"Then what you don't know, you have no reason to fear."

"Or I have every reason to fear it."

He grows quiet and I can't help but feel time slipping through my fingers like sand. "Please, Payne. We need them… *I* need them."

Payne screws his eyes shut and breathes out slowly. "... fine. Raise them. The rest... we'll deal with it... when it comes."

I press my hands into the ground immediately, pushing my power into the dirt until I can feel the potential for unlife prickling in the earth around Veseo and Nouille. I find the drumming of their power, their life force and it's waning. I cup it into my hands and will it into being. I will both men to sit up, for Nouille to smile at me. For Veseo to give me one of his joyful grins, the mirth sparkling in his eyes.

"Come back to me," I whisper.

It takes agonizing minutes as we sit there and I wonder if I've been successful. For all I know, maybe there are rules to this. Maybe you can only raise the dead once and that's it? But, I have to believe such isn't the case.

When they come alive at last, gasping and spluttering like swimmers coming up from the deep, the relief is so potent, I feel tears streaming down my face. Veseo is on his feet first, eyes wild and unfocused. Nouille merely groans and turns onto his side on the hearth rug, clutching his chest like it hurts to breathe.

"What the fuck just happened?" Veseo demands when he can find his voice again.

"You died," I say in a small voice. "My power… it's not enough to keep you alive. If I keep trying to animate you alone, you'll keep dying." I take a big breath, feeling like I'm going to lose my mind unless I can give birth to all the thoughts currently plowing through my mind. "I think... I think there's a way to keep you with us, but I… doubt you'll like it."

"I like it even less," Payne grumbles.

"There's nothing I won't do, short of fondling that knob." Veseo jerks a thumb at Payne as he says the words.

I bite my lip and wait to see if he'll put the pieces together. Eventually, he does.

"Oh, fuck me..."

I plan to, I think to myself, with an impish smile. "Payne needs to... share blood with all of us. Cement a bond so that we're all linked together. That's the only way we can all stay alive. We have to keep each other alive."

Veseo looks askance at Payne. "... Will I want to… or that is to say… will I have amorous feelings towards…" He swallows in obvious distaste.

Payne crosses his arms over his chest with a scowl. "I don't want to fuck you any more than you want to fuck me, beast."

Veseo snorts a laugh. "Likewise."

"Then we don't know if amorous feelings between... males is a byproduct?" Nouille asks.

I turn to face him. "We don't know."

"Are you sure it's the only way?" Veseo asks.

"It's the fastest way to ensure your survival," Payne nearly interrupts, still scowling at Veseo who scowls right back at him. "And it's the only thing we know that works."

"I say we do it," Nouille murmurs. "I... I want to remain alive, Veseo. I have to know if Herrick, Reve, and Malvolo are safe. I'll deal with lusting after the vampire... if it comes to that." He makes an expression that says he definitely hopes it doesn't.

There's an awkward moment where no one says anything more, the knowledge of what we're about to do crackling like lightning in the air. It can explode into violence or... other things at any second. When neither Nouille or Veseo move, I peel off my shirt, throwing it to the side. I've neglected to bind my chest for days now. It just makes things more difficult when Payne and I find a place to have sex. When we're alone together, all I want is to have him inside me.

Now I want all three men with equal fire. I can see the desire reflected in their eyes, though Nouille is trying hard not to look. Bashful, as always. It looks like I'll need to initiate. I scoot closer and gently take his hand, bringing it to one breast. A breath shudders out of him and he runs one thumb across my nipple, as if he can't help himself.

"Touch me, Nouille. Love me. I want to feel you inside me," I say, feeling the need to encourage him.

A full body shudder this time. "Briar... I..."

"Please?" And then I realize something and feel a lump in my throat. "I didn't… I didn't even think to ask either of you if you were… attracted to me."

"We are," Nouille responds immediately, obviously seeing the embarrassment overcoming me.

"That's not even a question," Veseo adds.

I just smile in response and in the next second, Nouille leans forward, wrapping his hands around my waist, pulling me onto his lap in a move so swift, I actually gasp. He's already hard, his cock straining against his trousers when I arrange my legs around his waist. He bucks up into me so I feel it, even through the barrier of my clothes. I'm a little nervous about having him inside me. He's larger even than Payne, whose length is nothing to sneeze at.

Speaking of, I look up at Payne, as if to ask if it's okay to proceed. He simply looks down at me and nods. When I look at Veseo, his eyes are already on me.

"I want you to focus on Nouille first," he says.

I just nod and return my attention to the more bashful of the two. His lips meet mine in a kiss so tender, it makes me want to weep. His hands are careful, treating me like I'm made of brittle glass and he might break me. His hands twine very gently in the hair at the nape of my neck. I press harder against him, taking control of the kiss. He moans a little when I skim his bottom lip with my tongue, then explore his tongue with mine.

"Briar..."

"Make love to me, Nouille."

He doesn't have to be told twice. He fumbles with the front of my trousers, almost popping the buttons off in his haste to get me naked. He disentangles me and lays me out on the hearth rug. Then he yanks my trousers down, growling a little with impatience when he has to remove my boots, as well. He takes a moment to drink me in when everything's off.

"Beautiful," he breathes, eyes roving over me. All of me feels warm, and I'm abruptly shy. Stupid, because I've been with Payne so many times now. I've been nude with a man before. But this is Nouille and he's looking at me like I'm some sort of goddess. Not to mention the fact that Veseo and Payne are both staring at us, as well. And when I glance down at their trousers, I notice they're both hard.

Veseo joins us, kneeling on the ground next to the fire. The fire traces his profile. I haven't noticed before, having only seen his hair by the light of the waning moon or the tiny pinpricks of starlight when the new moon came, but his hair isn't black. It's a red so dark, it appears black. Like the blood in Payne's veins, so sluggish it's turned dark with age. The deep red of Veseo's hair is oddly beautiful, edged in golden light.

Veseo begins a slow, leisurely exploration of my neck, decorating my collarbone with tiny bite marks. After weeks of Payne, the feeling of teeth on my bare flesh has me writhing, desire zinging straight to my core.

"Gods," I gasp.

I feel him pause, his mouth curving into a smile against the skin of my navel. He's working his way steadily lower, hands smoothing over my thighs, tracing the inner curve where they meet my sex. The ticklish sensation has me arching up against him. Eventually, he pins my squirming lower half to the floor, kissing my mound gently before he uses his fingers to part my folds. I guess what he's about to do the second before he does it.

His tongue skims through my folds in a motion so erotic, I almost climax from that alone. This isn't something Payne has ever done for me. Not because he doesn't wish to, but because his teeth grow sharper when he's aroused. Bloodplay is one thing, but he doesn't want to hurt me. It seems to frustrate him that he can't pleasure me in this manner. Even now, I can spy him from the corner of my eye, sitting just beyond the amber circle of firelight, eyes gleaming with frustrated lust. His cock is out, hard and ruddy with blood. I eye it, wishing it could be inside me now, too. Impossible, in all likelihood. I only have so many entrances, and he's needed for the second part of this endeavor,

All worry over Payne flies out of my head when Veseo latches onto one breast, tracing the aching bud with a dexterous tongue while palming the other, plucking at the nipple until I cry out.

Nouille has gone to work in earnest, finding the pearl at the apex of my sex, stroking over it with skillful motions. He's done this before. Perhaps with hundreds of women—it's obvious in the way he knows how to touch me, how to stroke me. He's had practice. I've heard that dragons are almost as long-lived as Fae. Damn near immortal, even if they're not invincible. Without outside intervention, they could possibly outlive my great-great-great grandchildren, looking just as they are now. Dragons freeze their aging once they reach their prime.

I'm a little envious of Nouille's other lovers. Was he this tender with them? Did he look at them the way he looks at me now, eyes burning with want and something more ardent still?

And Veseo... oh, Gods. The man knows his way around a woman's body! His hands wander, skillfully manipulating parts of me I had no idea could be erotic. He leaves small love bites on my body, imprinting a claim on me that few will be able to deny.

When Nouille begins pumping two fingers into me, my body shudders, bowing toward the ceiling as a climax hits me. My blood sings in my veins, body thrumming with bliss. I feel more alive than I ever have. Even the first time with Payne wasn't this good, because I can't feel him in precisely the same way I feel them. In them, there's a spark of me—an animating force that binds them to me more surely than any marriage rite. That spark calls to me, so that Nouille and Veseo moan, catching the aftershock of my orgasm.

"Fuck," Veseo breathes. "Don't do that, Briar."

"Do what?"

"I nearly just came in my pants," Veseo answers with a laugh.

"I think I speak for both of us that we'd rather spend our seed inside you, not on the floor," Nouille adds.

Veseo murmurs assent. He nuzzles my thigh like an overlarge cat, instead of the monstrous reptile I know he can become. It's incredibly endearing. He doesn't take his eyes off me as he shimmies out of his own trousers, cock springing free. My mouth goes a little dry. I've seen his manhood before, mostly flaccid just after he and his brother had climbed from their graves. It was impressive then. It's enormous now. I'm afraid he'll cleave me in two.

"Don't be frightened," he murmurs, clearly seeing the worry in my eyes.

"You're just so…" I swallow hard.

"It will fit," he answers with a chuckle.

Then he pulls his shirt off, discarding it beside his trousers. His physique resembles a chiseled marble statue. The firelight emphasizes every rippling muscle. I doubt there's an ounce of fat anywhere on his body. It's easy to forget that the tall dragon is a warrior. His biceps are hard, his torso firm, only a small smattering of hair leading down to the vee of his hips and the monster cock between.

"I won't hurt you," he says softly.

"I know. I believe you."

Nouille guides himself toward my entrance, the head of him brushing against my sex. He appears almost... shy. I smile at him, then take his cock in my hand, giving it a gentle squeeze. He lets out a shuddering breath, his eyes closing, mouth parting in pleasure. Then I guide him further inside so that the head of him is inside me. And that's all the encouragement it takes.

He thrusts himself into me with force I'd have never expected from him. I arch up underneath him and scream out my pleasure. There's also a slight pinch of pain as my muscles make way for his enormous width and length. But that pain is silenced a moment later as he starts to move within me. He's stretching me almost uncomfortably. Payne is sizable but not as long or girthy as Nouille. He gently pushes his brother away from my breasts, bracing one hand on the carpet near my head before rocking his hips into mine, setting a pace that's slow. It's what I need at the moment, as my body gets used to his size. He buries himself deep inside me, stroking a part of my core that makes me half-sob with pleasure.

Nouille closes his eyes, ecstasy stealing over his face. Small moans issue from his full, half-parted lips. Through him, I know what it's like to be inside me, the clench of my muscles around him as he drives in and out of me. The feeling is so dizzying, I almost see stars.

"Gods, Briar," Nouille breathes. "Oh, Gods."

I can feel his desperation, the need drawing his balls up tight as his climax approaches. He reaches between us with his free hand and begins stroking ardently at my pearl. Spikes of pure bliss tear through me and I scream as I climax.

Nouille follows not long after, panting my name. And that's when Payne strikes.

One moment he's across the room, stroking himself absently, watching as the other men have their wicked way with my body. The next, he's behind Nouille, drawing his head back by a hank of thick hair so that his neck is a perfect, taut line of muscle. With a savage snarl, Payne's head snaps forward and he drives sharp fangs into Nouille's throat.

Nouille lets out a short, surprised cry and bucks inside me. The thrust sends ripples of pleasure through me and I moan, despite the fact he's finished within me already. Through Nouille, I can feel Payne's teeth, the echoing ache blooming in my throat. Pain wars with the pleasure at being seated inside me so that the dragon's senses are thoroughly befuddled.

Payne doesn't drink for long, releasing Nouille after only a few swallows. He tears into his own wrist, jerking the skin away with a sound like tearing cloth. He presses the bloody appendage to Nouille's mouth. No bloody kisses for my dragons, it seems.

Nouille doesn't look pleased, but he takes the wrist and licks away the blood, not seeming to mind the taste. I suppose he *is* a dragon, even though his default state seems to be placid. Some part of his beast must be accustomed to the taste of blood.

I can feel it the second Payne's blood enters Nouille's system. It's like striking a chord on a lyre, a note that resonates with my own internal melody. He's connected to Payne, as Payne is to me. Our small triad hums in time with each other.

It seems high time to make it a quartet.

I shimmy from beneath Nouille, feeling a sense of loss when his length leaves me. I want to feel it again, over and over, as often as I can. But, now it's Veseo's turn. And I'm thrilled at the idea of feeling his length within me.

Turning onto my knees, I climb toward Veseo, who's stripped down before the fire. The flickering light dances in his eyes, so they seem to be aflame, urgent and lit with desire.

"How do you want me?" I ask, trying for a coy smile.

"Just like that," he breathes. "On your knees. I want to see the curve of your lovely back as I fuck you."

He reaches for me, spins me so that my back is to him. It gives me a view of Payne and Nouille, both watching us. Nouille with half-lidded eyes. I can only sense satiation from him. Perhaps a bit of drowsiness. Between the bloodletting and the lovemaking, he's exhausted, ready to succumb to deep, dreamless sleep. Payne is crouched over his shoulder, like some stone gargoyle, features made severe by the flickering light. His eyes are crimson and nearly feral.

Through Nouille I can sense something on the edge of Payne's mind. Something... wrong.

I don't have time to dwell on it, however. Veseo stretches his long, muscular frame over mine, pressing just the edge of teeth into my shoulder, before pushing himself into me. An involuntary gasp flies from my mouth as he seats himself fully inside. He's just as large as Nouille, but I can already tell he's not going to be gentle. Infectious joy seeps through the bond my necromancy forges between us. I can tell he'll fuck the way he lives—with abandon.

He threads long fingers into my hair, grabbing hold of it like it's a horse's reins. He withdraws just long enough to allow me to feel the loss of his hard length, before he rocks forward, thrusting so hard, he smacks against my ass with an audible sound. I moan, clenching tight. I'm already sensitive from Nouille's earlier ministrations, primed and ready for another climax.

"Touch yourself for me, Briar," he murmurs against my skin, after placing a searing kiss to the bite mark on my shoulder. "Stroke your pearl and find your pleasure. I want to feel your release clench hard around my cock."

"Yes," I breathe. It sounds like an excellent idea.

I have to raise up somewhat to follow the order, lest I fall. Veseo comes with me, never missing a thrust, even as I sit upright, almost sitting in his lap as he drives up into me. His hand releases my hair, instead curling around my hip for a moment, then tracing burning patterns up my stomach before clasping my right breast in one broad, calloused hand.

My fingers find my pearl, stroking it in frantic little motions. Whimpers ease out from between my lips, mostly variations of; 'Oh, Gods,' 'Yes,' and 'Veseo, Veseo, Veseo!'

I can feel Veseo's triumphant smile at the nape of my neck. I'm trembling all over. There seems to be a taut line drawn between my sex and the breast he's kneaded, because the second he plucks hard at the nipple, I'm through. I climax again, back arching away from Veseo, my breathless cry aimed at the bare rafters above.

Payne is gone from his position. Turned toward the fire, I don't see him strike at Veseo, just hear the slurp of thick liquid and the tearing of skin once more as Payne feeds his blood to Veseo. Awareness of all three tingles at the back of my skull. I can feel Nouille's honeyed torpor, the keen-edged satisfaction from Veseo. And then there's Payne.

He's weary. But at the edge of his awareness, there's a shadow. Something turbulent. A storm cloud of rage. My legs shake, unwilling to support my weight. I do the next best thing, lifting myself gingerly off Veseo, crawling awkwardly toward Payne. He's gone again in a too-quick movement. By the time I manage to find him again, he's lurking near the door, trousers on once again.

Payne cracks the door open, letting the sounds of the night pour in. Buzzing insects, the rustle of the wind, the far distant cry of a wolf.

"Payne..." I begin, unsure of what to say. He looks so remote, one would never guess at his anger.

"I need to hunt," he mutters. "I don't care for dragon blood."

And then, before I can answer, he ducks out into the night, letting the door snap shut behind him. I stare at the place he disappeared for a long time. What is this shadow over Payne? I can't escape the notion I've done something wrong.

We all agreed to this. It was the only way to ensure Nouille and Veseo's survival. Still, it couldn't have been easy for Payne to witness.

So, what in the name of Avernus can I do to fix it?

THIRTEEN
PAYNE

Something is very wrong.

All I see is blood.

For nights now, it's been growing worse and waking with the moon after the sanguine orgy of the previous evening, blood is all I can see. Crimson pooled in the shadows of the trees. The grass is garnet, the moon a claret disk in the sky. The thick lungfuls of air I drag in as we walk are tinged with the taste of copper and salt. My mouth is a desiccated wasteland, my throat attempting to close with every swallow, no matter how many squirrels, birds, or skunks I find to feed on in the surrounding woods.

What foul trickery is this?

Has Maura reneged on her bargain already?

Is this to be the wretched end of Prince Payne? If so, why now and not once Briar has completed her objective? Short-sighted of the Fae bitch, but then, faeries are such capricious creatures, at the best of times. Trust LeChance to wait twenty years before drawing my noose taut…

I'm staring doggedly at the lights of the town ahead, refusing to seek out the swan-like expanse of Briar's neck. If I spy it, I'm likely to attack. With my curse closing its fingers painfully around my throat, I'm sure to kill Lelita's daughter if I feed from her.

The dragon's blood was rich, zinging with power. It should have satisfied me. Instead, I was forced to flee in order to vomit the few mouthfuls I'd taken from each. Their blood tasted like day-old piss and I'd hunted until dawn to wash the taste away.

"Bite her," Tarquis all but croons into my ear as I watch her where she walks in front of me. *"Fuck her, take her, kill her."*

I jerk away from him, eyes wide and horrified. It's difficult not to answer him out loud. He grows more solid in my mind with every passing hour. It's almost as if the real Tarquis really is standing near me. If I speak out loud, if I respond to him, the others will think I'm mad. And if they think I'm mad, the dragons will kill me, even if it would result in their own deaths. They will do it to protect

Briar. They're already smitten with her. I can feel it through the link we share.

I also feel their suspicion towards me. I catch Veseo casting me distrustful glances over his shoulder as he walks. Nouille isn't immune either. They must sense the turmoil I face. If I confess the problem, they'll put me down like a rabid dog and leave Briar to fend for herself against one of the most dangerous creatures to ever set foot in Fantasia.

"I will not harm a hair on her head," I think back.

Tarquis' face twists up into an ugly sneer. *"Fool. You think yourself in love because she has her mother's face and she fucks like a talented whore? She's used you, you fool! She favors the dragons over you. You're just the mill wheel to keep them all going. Tear her throat out and die with a little dignity, Payne."*

"Shut the fuck up," I growl at the construct. *"And go away."*

He doesn't.

He keeps pace with me, his contempt a weight on my aching back as we crest the ridge that overlooks the City of Secrets. He glares daggers at the back of Briar's skull, muttering darkly about all the things he'd like to do to her. I feel the strangest urge to step between them, to protect her from the unseen phantom's fury. I have to catch myself. Remind myself that Tarquis can't do anything to her, except prod me to slake my thirst.

Briar reaches the top of the slope, hand in hand with Veseo and Nouille. Every time I see her dote on either man, the need for vengeance, for violence, grows. My nails are already biting bloody crescents into my palms with the effort it's taking not to attack. Seeing them silhouetted by the glimmering lights from the city below deepens the crimson hue that coats my vision.

I hate them.

I hate the fuckers so much, I want to pummel their faces in. I'm not sure what insanity possessed me to agree to bind them to us. Briar was *mine* and now she's tossing me aside like soiled clothing. What's more… they look right together. A matched set with the comparatively smaller woman between them. Where in this grouping is there room for the ruined prince?

All three of them stiffen in perfect synchronization.

"More capable than you," Tarquis observes. *"Just as strong and fleet-footed and they can fly. You are nothing, Payne. Kill the girl and end this farce."*

The hatred pulses so hard through me, I almost remember what it's like to have a heartbeat. My teeth ache so badly, I want to scream. Is this my punishment? To fall in love all over again and have her stolen by interlopers?

A very small, reasoned part of my brain tries to whisper that she hasn't truly chosen them over me. That she sought me out and kissed me upon waking this morning. I had been the one to wrench away from her, fearing loss of control.

That reasonable thought is almost impossible to make out over the beast inside that bays for blood.

Rip. Tear. Take what is mine.

"What's wrong?" I demand when the three of them stop short.

"They're already here," Veseo spits. "Vita's handiwork is piled up outside the town. Come and see."

Fuck you, my thoughts snarl. *Fuck you and your patronizing bullshit, Veseo! Choke on a cock and die!*

I inch forward, though following his directive feels like crawling over shards of glass on my belly. If the princess is truly happy with the dragon brothers, I'll find a place to end myself after we've finished here. It's not shocking that Maura LeChance has done this to me. The only mercy I can expect from her is the final death.

"Leave them all to die," Tarquis mutters. *"Why crawl after Briar like a cuckold, Payne? She doesn't want you."*

Even if that's true, I can't let her go into the city without my aid. Briar is Chosen, destined to save our land. It isn't just one princess on the line. It's the fate of a nation.

I crest the ridge and take up a position at Nouille's elbow. Of the two dragon brothers, he's the only one I can tolerate. At least he doesn't shoot his mouth off every other minute, like Veseo does.

Nouille gives me a sidelong glance and a frown as I crouch down low. I narrow my gaze on the streets below.

174

I can at least credit LeChance for one thing. A vampire's senses are almost as keen as a dragon's at night. The smell of copper and salt can't quite drown out the putrid stench that rises off the City of Secrets. It reminds me of the carnage left over from battle. It reeks of shit, piss, and moldering death. Blood, too, but I've been scenting that for days.

It doesn't take long to identify the source of the smell. They've been thrown one on top of each other until their wizened bodies form great stinking mounds at the borders of the city. Corpses. The only apparent cause of death for the lot of them is old age. But, given our experience in Nighburrow, we know that's untrue. The bitch goddess Vita has worked her magic here. I doubt there's a living soul in the City of Secrets and if there is, they won't be living for much longer.

Vita.

A goddess of life, to whom only one life is sacred—her own. Some adherents claim that the mere days one survives in her presence are worth the decades lost. I doubt it.

"You think she's aware we're coming?" I aim the question at Veseo, not bothering to look at the reptilian bastard, lest I give into the insistent urge to go for his eyes.

"It doesn't matter what I believe. Our mission is no less vital. We have to retrieve the Blue Faerie."

My eyes slide up to Briar. I can't see her beautiful eyes through the red. Why can I only see her painted in shades of blood? It's wrong. Fear allows me to swallow some of the bloodlust. It's painful and tastes like bile.

"Can you raise the Blue Fairie from here?" I ask.

Briar kneels, placing the fingertips of her right hand against the stubby grass. Her eyes flutter closed briefly and her face scrunches up with effort. Finally, her eyes snap open and she shakes her head.

"No, I don't think I can. I could raise every corpse in the city, save for the Blue Faerie. I feel a sort of... absence in the basement of... some place called the Hall of Oddities. I suspect she's there. Someone's probably warded it against my magic. I'll have to get closer."

"Perhaps you could raise the dead on the outskirts of the city," I suggest. "March them toward Vita while we charge the hall's defenses."

Veseo leans around Briar so he can sneer at me. "Yes, brilliant plan. Throw up a signal flare that we're here. They already know we're targeting the hall. Vita's forces will know to guard it more fiercely than they are currently. There are four of us, not four hundred! Our best chance at coming out of this with our ill-gotten lives intact is to do this stealthily."

I'm on my feet before I can think, the rage pulsing hot, blood on my tongue, teeth bared. In the second after that, I have Veseo by the collar. It takes everything I have to resist the urge to go for his thick jugular vein. He'll taste like piss, and even starving as I am, I don't want to sully my mouth with his blood.

Veseo is too slow to get his arms up to stop me and I slam a fist into his sternum so hard, I hear bone grind. He lets out a grunt of discomfort, more surprised than hurt. I know he can heal the damage quickly as a dragon shifter. Worse, he can shrug off even fatal damage for a time, due to Briar's magic.

"Payne!" Briar bleats. "What are you doing?"

My eyes are locked with Veseo's. "Condescend to me again, dragon. See what happens. It's my life essence that tethers you to her, that gives you life, you son of a bitch. I gave it to you and I'll take it away, you little pissant."

I want him to take a swing. Give me an excuse to tear his miserable throat out. Instead, he disentangles my hands from his shirt and pushes me away from him only hard enough to put distance between us.

"Fine. I apologize."

"Fuck you," I snarl in my mind.

"Kill him," Tarquis agrees. *"Rip his goddamn throat out."*

A soft, little hand alights on my shoulder and I whirl around, teeth bared. Briar shrinks back, eyes showing white. Her quiet voice is tight, worried.

"Payne, what's wrong? You're not acting like yourself."

Everything. Everything is wrong. But they'll kill me if I reveal just how pear-shaped things have gone. I can make it through one more day. Save the Blue Faerie. Get Briar a teacher. Then I can afford to die.

"Nothing," I mutter. Then I change the subject. "We need a plan. Has anyone got something worth proposing?"

"Well..." Nouille says slowly. He shuffles his feet sheepishly, looking for all the world like a schoolboy guilty of wrongdoing. Hard to believe he's a dragon sometimes. "I have an idea. But you won't like it."

"Tell us anyway," Briar sighs.

He tells us. And he's right. I hate it. It's just another layer of misery to be heaped on my night. Only Veseo looks amused.

"You're a sick fuck," I mutter as I glare at the bastard.

"So I've been told. When do we start?" Veseo asks.

I glance up at the claret disc of the moon. Even the stars seem to drip blood.

"Now," I sigh, defeated. "We're wasting moonlight."

FOURTEEN
BRIAR

I envy the others' ability to find oxygen superfluous. When I'm animate, I need to draw in breath. Which is unfortunate, when one is trapped under a layer of rotting bodies. I fear the reek will never leave my nose, no matter how hard I scrub myself later.

Granted, the dead aren't heavy. Whatever mechanism Vita uses to drain their life force, leaves them lighter than their frames would suggest. It's like being buried under a pile of leaves. Leaves that have turned gray, green, or black, and leak juices or foul-smelling gasses. The horrid miasma gathers beneath the tarp that's been slung over the cart, trapping us in with it. I'm fighting not to gag.

Nouille's idea to hide in plain sight was a good one. With so many dead being carted out of the city, we'll go unnoticed if we pose as corpses ourselves. Most of us don't have heartbeats. Still, it's rather disgusting in practice.

The fingers of each of my hands are clasped tightly by the men on either side of me. Veseo on my left, Payne on my right. As it was Nouille's idea, he's guiding the cart. He's the least volatile of us and the least likely to draw attention to himself. Yes, he's monstrously tall and that might draw some stares. But we'd reached a silent consensus after Payne's unwarranted attack on Veseo. Even though Payne is less likely to stand out, he can't be trusted. Not until we can get to the bottom of this strange, dark presence that looms over him.

Even now, Payne's face is a rictus, straining not to show whatever is roiling beneath the surface.

"Hold on," I urge him silently. *"We're nearly there."*

The cart hits a bump in the road and all the bodies atop us shift. The knobbly elbow of an elderly woman jabs into my throat and I make an unattractive "glerk" sound before I can control myself. The tarp shifts a little, as well, allowing just a hint of the outside air to waft inside. It's so sweet after the rot, it makes me want to weep.

I suck in as much air as I dare and hold it as long as I can. My lungs burn with the strain and even so, I don't want to risk more breaths. Many things that ally themselves with Morningstar and his generals have keen hearing. Who's to say one won't be guarding the House of Oddities? One false move and we'll all perish.

Veseo knocks an elbow into my ribs, just where the woman had before. My mouth opens in a silent cry and the air whooshes out of me, an almost explosive exhale in the silence. If my hands weren't pressed tightly to my sides, I might have retaliated. As it is, I can only twist my neck to glare at him.

"Breathe," he mouths.

I try, but it's difficult. Between the rot and the fear, I'm certain each inhale will be a dead giveaway. Nouille trudges along and through the gap I get a better look at our surroundings.

The City of Secrets looked forbidding, which only adds to the oppressive sense of fear. The buildings seemed to be constructed of ebony or darkly stained walnut. Unsurprising, given the dark wood that surrounds the city on almost every side. Still, at night, every building seems to loom above us, threatening. The torchlight that illuminates the pathway casts flickering shadows. At any moment, I expect something to juke out of them and attack. The windows of every building are dingy and warped. I wouldn't be able to spy a face behind the glass even if I had daylight to aid me.

Perhaps it would have been better if the tarp stayed secure. Foul but less frightening.

Veseo's hand squeezes mine tightly for a second, a silent assurance. He's letting me know he's here, that I'm not alone. He'll protect me. I doubt Vita and the others are prepared for a dragon assault. It calms me to know we can fly away from this cursed place the moment we have the Blue Faerie in hand.

The cart comes to a sudden and violent halt and the press of bodies roll over us in a malodorous wave. They settle most of their weight on Veseo and I, allowing Payne more range of motion than any of us have enjoyed for the last fifteen minutes. He uses it to roll onto his side and scoot away from us.

"I can't continue," he says in the barest whisper. "I can't remain under here, Briar."

There's a desperate, pleading note in his voice that I've never heard before.

"Hush," Veseo hisses. "Someone's coming."

And he's right. Not far away, a man's voice speaks. It's deep, like a bass rumble of thunder. The sound makes me shiver. Veseo clutches my hand even tighter, so hard it almost hurts. Perhaps I'm not the only one frightened.

"Halt," the voice orders. "Or feel Vita's wrath."

The cart is already still, crunching the gritty earth beneath us as it wobbles slightly in the wind. The section of tarp nearest us is beginning to lift in the light evening breeze. It's washing away the pungent corpse scent, which I'm grateful for. However, that scent is all that keeps us from being outed to Vita's people. She surely has shifters in her ranks. Payne and Veseo might pass through, but I'm sure I won't. They all claim magic has a scent and it clings to every part of me.

Nouille's voice drops in pitch, coming out almost as low as the newcomer's.

"Problem, sir?"

I can't see the man, but I can practically feel his anger. In my mind, I can see what Nouille sees and the man is short and ruddy-faced, blotchy patches of red speckling his skin like he's got some sort of choleric pox. His hands will be curled into meaty fists and his beady eyes will be searching for an easy target to swing at.

I'm not sure why he's choosing Nouille. Gentle as he can be, there's no denying Nouille's enormous in stature. He's trained every bit as hard as his brothers and though he prefers peace, he can and will fight. I don't think the baggy clothes he wears can hide that. Yet, the man doesn't seem to notice Nouille's strength and health. Perhaps it's the wad of stolen clothing we shoved beneath his shirt and cloak to give him the appearance of a hunchback. Nouille walks stooped over and perhaps the vision of him is believable enough. It had been the only costume we could come up with on short notice.

"That's Kiden of Ashaxe to you, peasant!"

Through our bond, I feel Nouille's temper stir. He's usually slow to anger and of the four of us, the least likely to quarrel, so I'm not sure what's provoked him. Maybe it's just the rude man? When Nouille speaks, his tone is dry and a little mocking, more like Payne's than anything I've ever heard from him before.

"Alright. Would you like me to call you Kiden or Mr. of Ashaxe?"

Veseo's grip really *does* hurt now. He wrings my hand like it's a sodden cloth he can't get dry. He seems unaware he's doing it, until I make a tiny, pained sound. It's all I dare do, and Nouille thankfully disguises it by leaning all his weight on one end of the cart, so it squeaks obnoxiously.

"Why you…" the man starts.

"I jest, sir," I can hear the forced smile in Nouille's voice. "I'm just tryin' to do what the mistress ordered. Can't have these bodies stinkin' up her city, can we?"

Kiden of Ashaxe says nothing and the only sound, save the wind, is the furious grinding of the man's teeth.

"What's beneath the tarp?" Kiden demands. He's spoiling for a fight and means to quarrel with someone, no matter the cause.

"Bodies, sir, as I said," Nouille replies, voice perceptibly tighter. "You know anything else that would stink half so much?"

Worry crackles through the air. Payne has scooted closer to me, something dark glinting in his eyes.

"Can't," he whispers again. "Can't wait… any longer. I'm sorry."

186

Veseo sits up just a fraction, anger flaring like the flames of a stoked fire. He wants to throttle Payne.

He never gets the chance, because three things happen simultaneously.

Kiden gets a grip on the tarp and flings the heavy burlap off in one flourishing movement, despite Nouille's attempts to stop him. Then the cart tips entirely, sending a cascade of bodies onto the road. Then Payne rolls me atop the corpses, straddles my waist, and lets out a feral, wolf's howl of pleasure.

His head snaps forward and he sinks long, deadly fangs into my throat.

FIFTEEN
VESEO

For a few stunned seconds, all I can do is stare at the vampire.

He rises up from the sea of corpses like a pale, marble statue, eyes blazing with garnet fire and I think he's going to leap on Kiden like a feral dog. It'll be messy and not as quiet as snapping the portly bastard's neck, but it will do.

Nouille is close and could snap his neck in one easy jerk. It's all the same, in the end. Kiden needs to die and join the pile of corpses. Not ideal, as someone will no doubt be searching for him, but it's workable. Once Kiden's dead, we'll travel on to the hall of Oddities, seize the Blue Faerie, and fly toward the Order of Aves. Maura has agreed to meet us there.

But that plan crumbles like a moist pastry when Payne lunges, not for Kiden, who's staring at us in open-mouthed shock, but at *Briar*. Payne's head snaps forward in a deadly

viper's strike, burying his fangs into her throat.
A growl trickles from his lips, muffled by the
column of his throat. At that moment, he looks
like a rabid animal, reason gone, capable of
only savagery.

Payne's jaws work, moving like he's trying
to chew through a particularly thick piece of
mutton. My stomach lurches as Briar's pain
spikes through me. It's a one two punch of
physical agony and a mental scream of
betrayal. She can't force an actual cry from her
lips. He's trying in earnest to crush her larynx
before he tears her throat out.

Kiden lets out an indignant cry, which,
absurdly, is what manages to break Nouille and
I from our frozen shock. Without consulting
each other, we each pick a target. Nouille
lunges for Kiden, who's letting out a parrot-like
squawk of; "Intruders! Mistress Vita there are
intruders! Mistress…"

Nouille stands up to his full height,
shrugging off the cloak and the bundle of
clothes on his back. Then he shoots an arm out,
catching Kiden around the neck like a
Shepherd's crook. He only has to wrench hard
to the right once. Kiden's neck snaps with a
sound not unlike a nutcracker crushing a

walnut. A little meatier, perhaps, because it's encased in flesh. But the sound is close.

Meanwhile, I go for Payne, seizing him by the back of the neck like he's a misbehaving kitten. Wrenching him back completely might kill Briar. A vampire's bite is dangerous at the best of times and this one is clearly aiming to maim or kill.

It reminds me of something I was told by one of Delerood's best captains. We'd spoken during my family's time aboard the *Serpent's Bane* during the war. Or rather... the last war. It feels weeks, not decades, old to me. Perhaps that's why I recall it so acutely.

The best way to deter a shark is to hit the snout or gills.

A vampire isn't a shark obviously, but perhaps if I can get his teeth out of her the damage may be minimal. So I cock my fist back, and drive it forward in a swift jab, right into Payne's Adam's apple.

The funny thing about the mind is, it will still respond to stimulus it accepted in life, even when the body is dead. Payne doesn't need air, but his mind still sends a panicked impulse to his body saying otherwise—something I feel strongly through the bond we share. He reacts to the strike with a choked sound and rocks back, teeth sliding out of Briar's flesh with a slick, slurping sound. His teeth drip scarlet, his lips coated in blood.

The second she's free of him, I watch Nouille go for Briar, which means I'm free to go after Payne. I drive him down onto the pile of corpses and rain down blows. His nose cracks immediately. It doesn't fountain blood in that satisfying way living bodies do. When Malvolo and I brawled in earnest, the first to snap the other's nose was usually considered the win. Our mothers would maul us both if we managed to actually maim the other seriously.

Payne's blood is sluggish, running like mafic lava, slow and unhurried. He sucks in a pained breath and I hit him again, rattling his teeth, splitting his lip, and drawing an actual cry from him. It's not enough. The rat bastard has only done one thing worth lauding the entire trip. He's selfish, hoarding Briar like... well like a dragon. Selfish and secretive. But even the most avaricious among my brothers could still share his women. The darkness in Payne disturbs me and now? It's dangerous.

"I'll fucking kill you, you son of a bitch!" I yell at him.

It may end me as well, but I'll take a million years in the void to preserve Briar's life. Her magic binds me to this world, but it isn't her magic that draws me to her. It's the tenderness of her heart. The compassion she extended Payne, even with all he's done to ruin her. He doesn't deserve it, any of it. And now, he's going to die.

My ears are ringing, rage whipping like shrill winds, drowning out the outside world in lieu of a pulse. Maybe that's why I don't hear her cries, at first. I do feel the tug on my arm, though against my strength, it feels like the feeble attempts of a child. When I glance back at Briar, I find her leaning all her weight against me, trying to push me back.

"Veseo, no!" she pants, holding a hand to her throat where her blood still bleeds through her fingers. Nouille tries to pull her away so he can tend to her wound but she shirks him away.

"Please stop!" she yells to me.

"He tried to kill you, Briar!"

Briar points a shaking finger in Payne's direction. "Look at him, Veseo. Really *look.*"

I follow the line of her finger toward Payne's prone form. There's a large, seething part of me that wants to ignore her plea and turn Payne's head into a mush of gray matter and bone fragments. It's alarming, because I haven't felt battle rage like this since Nighburrow, where I met my end. It's not my nature. I enjoy a spirited bout with my brothers or any of my comrades in our battalion but not this... fury.

I swallow back the bloodlust and peer closely at him. He's still thrashing, teeth bared, eyes as crimson as the blood on his lips. There's no reason in those eyes. They seem faintly glazed. I've seen that expression before.

"Gods," I breathe. "He's bespelled!"

"Bespelled by what?" Briar breathes, finally allowing Nouille to tend to her throat.

"Is she..." I start, looking to my brother.

"She will be fine," he says with a curt nod.

I feel relief suffuse me as I turn to face her again in order to explain. "They used to call it the Bacchanal. It's a mixture that causes bloodlust and madness. It usually kills the host."

"But he's already dead," Nouille murmurs as I nod, my attention turning to Kiden's limp body where it lays in a crumpled heap on the ground. His neck is twisted at an almost ninety degree angle. The man's eyes stare sightlessly forward, mouth still open in a cry of warning.

"How did they get it into him?" she whispers.

"I don't know," I mutter, glancing up and down the street. Someone has to have heard Kiden's cry of warning and will be coming to end us at any moment.

I slide off the pile of bodies, boots hitting solid ground, moments later. Briar is balanced precariously atop the pile and I motion for her to leap. She gives the ground a look of frank trepidation.

"I'll catch you." *I will always catch you.*

Briar swallows convulsively and then nods, a quick jerky bob of her head. She leaps from the heap and sails a short way down. I'm ready, arms extended. She lands a moment later, her welcome weight comforting me more than I expect. She's alive... mostly. And when she curls into me contentedly, my dead heart swells.

Mine. My mate.

Nouille's as well. Probably Payne's too, but not for long if he attacks again. Bespelled or not, I *will* end him if he goes for her ever again.

"Take Payne," I call over to Nouille. "Let's see if we can find a way to cure the useless lout."

"Veseo," Briar chides.

I ignore her. We can argue about the merits of the prince at a later date. For now, we must get to the Hall of Oddities before...

A shout goes up behind us, quickly followed by the thunder of heavy feet.

Before *that*.

Vita's forces are coming and, if my senses don't lead me astray, there's at least a dozen sets of feet beating a path toward us. Nouille and I don't have to say a word. We exchange one glance and then break out into an all-out gallop, only slowing to take turns into the narrow alleyways between the houses. The heavy footfalls belong to large pursuers. We can avoid the heavy combatants if we're clever and fast enough.

Payne is still thrashing, fangs extended farther than I've ever seen them. they look more like protruding tusks. They've become so large, he can't close his lips around them. They're cutting at his lips and chin, more blood slopping slowly down his front. His jaw is grinding oddly.

"He's going to snap his own jaw," I say, my ire disappearing as I watch the prince transform before my eyes. Every so often he lets out an animal whimper. He's clearly in agony.

His ruined nose pops back into place with a sickening crunch of bone, then telescopes forward to form a snout. The skin strains so tightly, I fear it will tear.

"Fuck," I swear.

Bacchanal is a sort of poison. Much like the bloodwine Bacchus created, it drives the user mad with killing rage. The difference is the effect on the body. With bloodwine, only the mind goes. Bacchanal transforms the very body. Sometimes those who are very unfortunate change into shapes they aren't meant to take. For shifters, it isn't always immediately fatal. Our bodies are used to reforming, even if the Bacchanal often makes us turn into something different than we're used to. It's the transformation that will drive us into a rabid frenzy that eventually stops the heart.

That was what had happened to our shared lover, Peregrine, years ago. A female huntsman, from House Accipitrine, Peregrine was killed in a battle with the Great Evil, and

Bacchus specifically. The shift forced her into the last shape she'd been in contact with—a dragon. The sudden and unfamiliar shift into a too-large shape literally torn her apart.

I believe that's what's happening to Payne now. His body is trying to twist into whatever he last hunted. From the beady black of its eyes and the shape of the snout, I'd say that creature was a boar.

"What's happening to him?" Briar squeaks. "Can we stop it?"

I've never seen it reversed. If he ate something in the last few days that had been dosed, I'm astonished he's held out this long. Perhaps it's because his blood doesn't circulate. Alternatively, it could be Briar's magic holding it at bay. Whatever the reason, it's clearly not working now. If Payne dies, it's only a matter of time before the rest of us perish, as well. Without proper training, Briar can't keep herself or the rest of us animate. She'll keel over one day, like a possum in the face of a predator, and she'll be killed. Permanently.

"We'll have to," I reply grimly.

My only hope is that we can find something in the Hall of Oddities that can save the prince and, likewise, save us.

A voice like shifting gravel speaks and I jerk in surprise. The sound comes from Payne's mouth, but it's not the mellifluous tone I'm familiar with.

"Beastly acts deserve beastly ends," the thing croons. Or as much as a voice like tumbling rocks *can* croon. "This is justice."

Briar leans out of my arms and shoves her face near Payne's.

"I will end you, Bacchus," she hisses. "Mark my words."

Payne's eyes, still crimson, glitter with malice. "Good luck, deadling."

A crash just behind us draws my attention to the alley we've just exited. My stomach lurches, because my dead heart can't.

A giant is attempting to force its way through the streets, sometimes just stepping *over* buildings. It's one of the smallest I've ever seen, though it's still leagues taller than any human or shifter in living memory. Twenty meters, instead of the usual fifty or sixty. It's difficult to see its shaggy head from where we stand. If it catches up, it's likely to smash us like roaches beneath its heel. We need to get to the Hall of Oddities. Vita's men aren't likely to destroy it, even with us inside. They value the

Blue Faerie's body too much to destroy it. Her pixie dust can cause forgetfulness and make it easier to brainwash their followers.

There's a high, jubilant laugh from far above us. I crane my neck and find a small, human-like shape on the giant's enormous shoulder. She looks like a pixie in comparison, but she's not Fae.

She's breathtakingly beautiful at first glance. Long, leaf-green hair arranged in a loose braid. Someone has woven ribbons and wildflowers into it. She looks, for all the world, like a Mayfair queen. Her perpetually golden skin reminds me a bit of Herrick's, an association I don't want to make because it reminds me that I don't know if my brother is dead or alive. Her dress is short, but flowing, the perfect blue-green of coastal waters. I know, without being able to glimpse them, that her eyes are oaken brown.

Fuck, fuck, fuck.

"Vita," Nouille whispers just behind me, horrified.

"Vita?" Briar repeats, fear making the question almost breathless. She tries to spy the goddess, but her mostly human eyes can't strain far enough to make her out clearly.

I press on, drawing speed from somewhere deep inside me. My muscles burn, my breath slicing at my lungs like knives. We have to get into the Hall. *Now.*

Thirty yards.

Twenty.

Ten.

The giant's foot is hurtling down at us. Taking a chance, I push off the ground with all my strength and go sailing sideways, avoiding the huge, bunioned feet of the giant by inches. A million splinters dig into my skin as we crash through. I curl my body around Briar's, protecting her from the wooden shrapnel flying all around us.

My back hits the glass of a cage and shatters it, letting a furry creature run free. Nouille tumbles in, as well, pinning Payne to the floorboards. Outside, all is silent.

I glance around, amazed at the creatures hopping, slithering, or flitting back and forth in cages. Paintings leer down at us, mirrors reflect back our battered countenances, and baubles swivel to and fro on magicked pedestals. The nearest is a brassy oil lamp that shimmers lightly in the low light.

We've made it.

The Hall of Oddities.

Now we have to find a dead faerie in this mess, reverse the spell on the prince, and stymie a goddess intent on killing us all.

Simple.

Right.

SIXTEEN
NOUILLE

I snatch the first length of cord I can find.

Payne seems momentarily stunned by the violent fall into the Hall of Oddities, giving me a respite. During the panicked flight over, he'd managed to gore my throat with his rapidly growing tusks. If I'd been a normal, living man, I'd be dead. As it is, my blood runs inky dark down my skin, the consistency of pitch.

Some of it drips into Payne's face as he begins to stir. The cord doesn't look like much. A few feet long and as thin as the cord on a coin purse. It's dotted with around forty beads, interspersed with knots, feathers, and chicken bones. It seems deceptively fragile at first glance. But, I know better. It's a witch's ladder, a relatively common charm in the days pre-war. Though not now. I hear that all nations but Delerood hold a staunch anti-magic stance over a decade later. Absurd.

I lodge a boot under Payne's ribs and pin him to the floor as I seize first one hand and then the other. The witch's ladder ought to at least slow the spread of the Bacchanal, even if it can't stop it outright. The Blue Faerie will have answers for us after she's raised... I hope.

Payne lets out a shriek and bucks as the bone spurs dig into his wrist. Briar twists in Veseo's arms, craning to see what's been done to him. I regret his pain, of course. As choleric as his temper can be at times, he is a warrior and his devotion to Briar is paramount. When he's sane, that is. Only Veseo dislikes him and I believe that dislike is owing to the fact that he's so like Malvolo that they're destined to clash. Veseo will come around eventually, if Payne lives.

"Don't hurt him," Briar breathes. "Please, Nouille."

I can't pause to whisper assurances to her. Explanations will take time we don't have. Furthermore, Briar needs to focus on her own healing. Luckily, we were able to find a spare sheet which we ripped into bandages in which to bind her neck. After holding pressure to the wound for a few minutes, the blood appeared staunched, but the Blue Fairie will need to address Briar's wounds, just as she'll need to address Payne's.

For now, I need to plug the hole in the wall before Vita and her acolytes can swarm inside and kill us all. Casting around to find something large enough to stymie them for more than a moment or two, I find my answer in a large clothespress. The paint flakes off in my hand as I scoot it in front of the hole. The tag angling from its handles reads:

'Ensouled Armoire, 1000 Gold Pieces to purchase.'

"Sorry," I murmur to it. "Please forgive me, but we have to escape."

The armoire creaks and a wispy male voice seems to echo from the interior. "You are kind, stranger. I will stand guard."

I blink at it once in surprise, before nodding my thanks. I pat its side, as though the thing has shoulders, and then set off down the row. Payne's strength seems to be waning, because he's flopping like a landbound fish, instead of thrashing like a terrier with a rat.

"Up, Payne," I say, hauling him to his feet, though I'm supporting most of his weight.

It's awkward and we knock into a nearby pillar, toppling an oil lamp. Reflexively, I stoop to pick it up. My fingers tingle upon contact with the brassy surface. Magic. This thing is

definitely enchanted. I attach it to my belt loop
for safekeeping and shuffle forward as quickly
as Payne's dead weight will allow.

Veseo is already sixteen feet ahead and it's
a struggle to catch up to him. Briar has at least
regained her feet and Veseo is leaning close,
fussing over her wound. He reminds me of
Herrick, with his soft fingers and probing
questions. Herrick always said Veseo had the
temperament to be a healer. Unlike Malvolo,
who'd likely smother patients the moment he
got sick of their winging.

Briar bats his hand away. "I'm fine, Veseo,
really. It doesn't hurt."

"It's deep.

"Don't fuss with the bandages, Veseo," I
say to him.

"If Payne hit any arteries, I'd be dead,"
Briar says. It could be worse. Let's go."

"Briar..."

She tries to turn away, but Veseo shoots out
a hand to stop her. He gently cages her against
what looks like a carnival mirror. It's warped
so he looks as tall as the giant outside for a
moment. He runs his fingers along the side of
her neck, pressing them firmly over the portion
of her skin Payne savaged. Veseo's brow

furrows in concentration and his essence just seems to... flicker.

Briar gasps and she shoves at his hand. When it comes loose, her throat is smooth and unblemished. I have to admit, I'm as shocked as she is.

"What in the name of Avernus was that?" she demands.

"Energy," Veseo says with a shrug. "Mine, specifically. We're all bound and your magic gives us life. I figured it was only fair I returned some of it to you. And... it would appear it worked, didn't it?"

"Good thinking, brother," I say with a quick nod.

Veseo smiles at me as Briar smacks his bicep, eyes wide and glassy with tears. "Don't waste your life energy again! I wasn't even hurt that badly! You could have drained yourself back to the afterlife, you loon!"

"You'd be worth it."

The words thrum with conviction and resonate with me. For once, I think, Veseo, Payne, and I are in complete agreement. (Or would be, if Payne weren't going mad.) Our unlives are a worthwhile trade to keep Briar safe.

The tears spill over and she swipes at them furiously. "I'm not."

"Don't argue," Veseo says, his trademark grin appearing on his face, though it's a touch strained. "It's unseemly for a princess."

She smacks his bicep again. "You're a… a cock."

Veseo's smile grows, completely unrepentant. "But you love me."

She grows quiet for a moment and breathes in deeply. I can see Veseo's eyes on her, as awaiting her response. I have to admit, I'm curious as to her feelings towards the two of us, as well. It's quite clear she loves Payne, but I'm not certain how deeply her feelings run for my brother and me.

"I do," she whispers. "I love all three of you."

It feels like a drop of warm sunlight hits my belly, stoking the fires of my dragon. I will go anywhere, endure anything for this woman.

The building quakes and outside, I can hear the giant's roar. There are more voices, including the high, reedy tone of Vita. Briar speaks for all of us when she mutters;

"We need to go."

She's right. The brave spirit trapped in the armoire won't last forever. We wind our way through the narrow corridors, passing more mirrors, which Veseo tips to block our exit. There are more objects, whirring, puffing or letting out shrill cries. The din disguises our hasty retreat nicely. I stare at a squat tank full of glowing green water. The pickled body of a siren floats near the surface, eyes wide and unseeing.

Barbarians.

I'll bet Vita put this one in the hall as a punishment. No one deserves to have their body gawked at in such a fashion, no matter the crime. This one has almost certainly been killed for treason. As if Morningstar has any right to give commands or accuse people of heresy. He's the invader here.

There are more bodies, the further we travel and we're forced to slow to examine each. A small blonde who appears to have had her eyes pecked out by a large bird, the golden cascade of her hair so long and thick, it's been used as her shroud. A lion curled around a cub, who almost appears to be sleeping. A pegasi and rider. A squat little man that appears to have been stuffed and holds a bundle of spun gold in one hand.

The Blue Faerie is conspicuously absent.

It isn't difficult to spy a perished Seelie. They don't rot, as such, but the body begins to produce pheromones uncontrollably. In theory, it ought to invite the earth to swallow her whole and spawn new life. Entire forests spring up around the body, fueled by the life-giving power. It's how the Enchanted Forest sprang into being. The mother of the fabled Tinkerbell perished during the war and was swallowed by the earth. Not long after, the beautiful silver forest rose up, practically overnight.

Unseelie deaths are the opposite. Unseelie bodies produce curses and drain life and sanity anywhere they are unfortunate enough to perish. It's rumored the Forest of No Return was spawned by the Unseelie Queen's demise. Her consort, Septimus, staged a coup for the throne, in exchange for his loyalty when the Great Evil began to spread over our lands. Fae are matriarchal by nature and without either queen, the balance of power is incredibly skewed.

"Gag Payne and stop that infernal clinking at your waist, Nouille," Veseo hisses.

The shock of the fall has worn off and
Payne is snarling again. The corpse displays are
far from the noisy front of the hall and the noise
is sure to attract the attention of Vita's people.
The distant splintering of wood and the chorus
of voices that follow means they've finally
made it past the armoire. I feel a momentary
pang for the soul trapped in the wooden shell. I
send a quick prayer to the gods of our people.

*Give him a good afterlife. He was a good
soul.*

I whip my shirt off, in lieu of anything else
to use as a gag, wad it up, and shove it into
Payne's open maw. It muffles the snarls—but
only just. I can't help the smile that hits my
mouth. I wish I could have done this to Payne
on more than this occasion…

We reach the back wall, which is almost
startling in its blandness after the trek through
the oddities. I scour the surface, looking for
anything that might constitute an exit. There
has to be a door somewhere. The architects
wouldn't allow for only one doorway. The hall
would become a firetrap, especially with all the
smoking and hissing oddities near the front.

I spy the door near the seam where the front
wall meets the side. A small, almost

imperceptible notch in the wood, only large enough to squirm a finger or two inside. A human would overlook it, but not a dragon's keen eyes. A hidden entrance?

"Stand back," Veseo mutters. "I'll make an exit."

"No. Wait just a moment," I say.

He turns to give me a baleful stare. "We don't have time."

"Just a few seconds, Veseo. I think I've found something."

I shoulder my way past Veseo. The voices are growing louder. Animals squawk as their cages are toppled. China and mirrors break with tinkling sounds that echo back to us. It appears Vita's people are planning to go *through* the exhibits, not around them. I worm my fingers into the notch and am gratified when a latch clicks. It's a simple matter to shoulder the door open and peer down.

The scent hits me immediately.

Sweet, hanging in the air like the candied floss one could find in Sweetland. It's supposed to smell differently from person to person. There's a hint of Briar's scent, the musty smell of my cave, the ozone just before a lightning strike.

"She's down here," I say triumphantly. "Come on"

I start down the stairs, determined to put my body before Briar and Veseo's if there's a guard at the bottom of the rickety wooden steps. Payne settles a little as the scent washes over him, as well. Does he scent Briar as I do? Briar, blood, and the char of a campfire? It's the only thing he's admitted to enjoying in recent weeks.

Somehow I don't think there's a guard patrolling this place. Below, everything is as silent as the grave. The lamp clinks when we reach the bottom and Briar's eyes dart down to it. They go round and her lips twist into a bright, and unexpected smile.

"Nouille, you're brilliant!"

"Of course he is," Veseo says, almost offended on my behalf and then; "Why is he brilliant?"

"The lamp! It's a djinn's lamp! Maura covered them in my lessons!"

"What does it do?" Veseo asks.

"They grant wishes!"

I stare down at the brassy oil lamp at my waist. I hadn't really thought about much besides trading it for supplies, if we made it

212

out. It was the closest thing nearby that looked valuable.

Veseo slams the door shut and braces his back against it, so that our pursuers can't push their way in easily. Ideally, he could shift, blocking it as surely as the giant could. But, this room is too cramped to even perform a partial change.

"While I've not heard of their lamps, I do know the Djinn are dangerous," Veseo growls. "They're Hassan's people."

"Why does that," Briar starts as he interrupts.

"You rub that lamp and there will be consequences. Possibly fatal consequences."

"It's our only hope," Briar says as the heavy stomp of boots sounds above our heads. "And some Djinns are benign. Maura taught me that."

Like Unseelie are bastions of truth and goodwill.

Maura LeChance, no matter how helpful she's been to the cause, is still dark Fae. Her definition of benign likely differs from ours. Still, Briar is right. There's no way out of the chamber. Besides, Payne is growing more boar-like by the second, even with the witch's ladder affixed to his wrists. Not only that, but sunrise is coming, and that will render us all unconscious, provided Payne is still alive in the next fifteen to twenty minutes.

"Do it," I say. "I'll retrieve the Blue Faerie."

She's settled into a trough of some sort. She's been laid out on golden straw, the same sort the squat man upstairs was clutching. She doesn't even take up half the space. The royal caste of the faeries are surprisingly small. Only three or four feet tall, though their proportions aren't dwarf-like. She used to be called Saxe, to those of us who knew her, before she succumbed to this awful fate. To the masses, she's the Blue Faerie and always will be, and it's not a wonder. Her hair is teal, her skin a cyanic hue, like she's reflecting a cloudless sky. If they were open, her eyes would be indigo. And her gowns are always aquamarine and glittering with jewels.

Every part of her is glittering now.

The pheromones ooze out of her as pixie dust, shining a white that's painful to look at. Someone has been hacking at the weeds that sprung up beneath her, ensuring her body stays out of touch with the earth she so desperately wants to return to.

"Just a little longer, Saxe. Then you can rest for good," I murmur, lifting her limp form from the trough. Her pixie dust swirls off her body, teasing my nose until I sneeze. To my surprise, the moment the droplets find the floor, flowers spring up.

Seelie Fae are the strangest creatures.

Meanwhile, Briar is busy chafing the sides of the lamp. She stares at it hopefully, as though it holds the answer to our every problem. It might. Or perhaps it will only fuck us in the ass a little more firmly.

It takes thirty excruciatingly long seconds for the lamp to respond. Then a plume of red-orange smoke jets from the spout, like a kettle that's hit its boiling point. The smoke rapidly fills the air around Briar, swaying in place for a moment, until it can solidify. I want to jerk her away from the smoky image, half expecting it to resolve into the tall, darkly-tanned form of Hassan.

Instead, the djinn is a short, slender woman, barely bigger than Saxe herself. She has the same complexion as Hassan, but that's the where the similarities end. Where his hair is dark, this woman's is ginger. Her eyes glow amber, a contrast to the floor-length black dress she wears. Orange stitching stands out at the collar and waist.

She smiles thinly at Briar. "Hello, Mistress. I am called Rajah. I will grant you wishes thrice and no more. What do you ask of me first?"

Briar opens her mouth, closes it, and bites her lip in thought. Clever girl. Djinn are very literal. One false word could lose her a wish. Or bring her something she doesn't want at all.

"Can I wish for the death of someone?" Briar asks.

The djinn looks at her. "I cannot grant death, nor life."

"I was going to ask to end Morningstar," Briar says in explanation to me. I just nod, thinking it would have been a good wish.

"I apologize, mistress, but a djinn does not hold that sort of power. Only a Shepherd does," Rajah says.

Payne bucks and moans as bristles start to protrude from his newly formed snout. He huffs out rapid breaths, each sounding more bestial than the last.

"He's been dosed with Bacchanal," Briar says to the genie. "I'd like him healed, please."

216

She can't seem to help the polite addendum, though it isn't necessary. The djinn has to respond. They're compelled to. Morningstar has permanent hold on Hassan through one of his wishes, securing an ally for life, whether Hassan wants that or not. It occurs to me Briar could do the same. I doubt her conscience could bear the thought of enslaving this djinn. Briar's heart is tender and it's one of the many things I love about her.

"Done," Rajah purrs.

A flash of vivid light sears my eyes and when the spots clear, I find Payne on the floor, panting and wild-eyed with panic, but obviously hale and hearty once more. Or as hearty as a corpse *can* be.

Briar's eyes brim with grateful tears and she turns to give the djinn a tremulous smile. "Thank you."

Rajah cocks her head curiously. "Your gratitude is unnecessary, Mistress. I am here to serve."

"Of course it is," Briar says, swiping at the tears on her cheeks. "You don't deserve to be beholden to anyone, Rajah."

The genie thinks about Briar's words for a moment. Briar continues when it appears Rajah is at a loss for words. "In fact... when you've taken us all elsewhere... do not return to your lamp. Do not grant wishes. Do what *you* wish."

Rajah blinks, face vulnerable and uncertain. "Mistress?"

"Briar," she corrects. "Take us to my godmother, Maura LeChance, and when you are through, be a slave no more. Those are my wishes."

The door bucks violently, shoving Veseo off his feet. He staggers and almost hits the opposite wall.

"Now, please," I urge.

Rajah smiles, claps her hand together once, and then light sears my eyes once again. Our surroundings stream together like wet paint. The last thing we hear is Vita's indignant shriek as we disappear entirely.

SEVENTEEN
BRIAR

We tumble, choking and spluttering, onto the rug before Maura's fire.

The air in the Hall of Oddities had been cold and thin, so it feels like sucking in a lungful of pudding to find myself back in Maura's warm, thickly perfumed chambers. I gasp in several breaths before trying to sit up. It's difficult, as Payne has landed awkwardly across me.

When he realizes what's happened, he rolls off me. I roll with him, choking on relief. I'm half-straddling his waist and I don't care that the others are watching. I cup his face in both hands, cradling him like he's the most precious thing in the world to me.

His face has reverted back to its natural state, strong and chiseled. His eyes still look a bit wild, but soften when he catches sight of me above him. A fat teardrop splatters onto his cheek, then another.

Payne smiles faintly and lifts a hand to stroke my cheek. "Don't cry, Briar. Everything is going to be alright."

"I almost lost you!" I sob as I turn to face Veseo and Nouille. "All of you. It was so close." I face my prince again. "Don't ever scare me like that again!"

Payne collects me in his arms and holds me tightly. "Briar," he starts. "I don't even know how to apologize to you…"

"Don't," I interrupt him with my fingers above his lips. "You weren't in your right frame of mind. And, besides, none of that matters now."

The panic of the last few minutes still grips me tight, but my body is relaxing by degrees. It's finally starting to sink in that I'm safe. We're all safe. Not only that, we've accomplished what we set out to do. We have the Blue Faerie's body and we're in the safety of Maura's home.

I crane my neck, just to be sure we really did make it back with the Blue Fairie and there she is. Her limp body is slumped over Nouille. He's covered from head to do with shining white dust. It's almost cute and the scent rolling off him is intoxicating. The woodsmoke scent

220

of my dragon men, the salt and copper of
Payne, the smell of fresh spun wool and the
dust motes that stirred in Bloodstone Castle. It
wraps me in a warm cloak of nostalgia.

"Well, that's a development," Maura
murmurs from behind us. If I twist, I can see
her.

She's dressed in a gown of black silk that
almost blends with the darkness of her skin.
Her violet hair is loose and tousled, like she's
just rolled out of bed. On her face is a look of
soft bewilderment.

"Maura!" I say as I run to her and she
engulfs me in her arms.

"I'd expected him to fall for you. I never
expected you to reciprocate," she says as she
faces Payne.

"Maura," Payne greets her.

"You've done well, Payne," she says. "I
suppose you want me to hold to my end of the
bargain and release you from your curse?"

I look at him and he looks at me. I don't
know what it will mean for our bond if Maura
releases him and turns him human again. Our
bond is owing to our undeath—how each of us
share that same feature. If Payne becomes
human again…

"Actually, I've reconsidered," he answers as he smiles at me.

"Interesting," Maura comments.

"Payne, this is something you've always wanted," I argue.

He shakes his head. "Not as much as I want you, princess."

"Interesting, indeed," Maura comments and then turns to Veles, offering him an amused expression. And speaking of Veles...

The huge dragon has climbed to his feet, eyes wide, face pale like he's seen a ghost.

"Veseo? Nouille?"

Both dragons sit up at the sound of their names, Nouille gently setting the Blue Faerie aside so he can see properly. When their heads swivel to face Veles, they look equally shocked.

Veseo is the first to speak and his voice comes out as a croaky whisper. "Father?"

Father? Veles is their father?

I feel the need to scramble to my feet and bow or... something. My cheeks flame as I realize I've made love with both of his sons. He's been Maura's mate for as long as I've known her. I've always considered him a father figure because I was never able to meet my

222

own. Now, I'm in a four-way bond with his sons and the vampire prince he despises. What must he think?

But Veles only has eyes for his sons at the moment. He drinks them in for several long seconds, roving over their bodies to see they're whole. Then his gaze flicks over to Payne and me, taking in the way we've all oriented around each other. We've drifted together unconsciously, so that each one of them is touching a part of me. Veseo's hand on the small of my back, Nouille's shoulder to my shoulder, Payne's thumb tracing the pulse on my wrist.

Veles throws his head back and lets out a braying laugh. It's so loud and sudden, I startle, moving closer to Payne. I get the uncomfortable feeling I'm the butt of a joke, but I don't know the punchline. Should I be offended?

"Gods, you two as well?" he says when the laughter dies down to a chortle.

Nouille frowns, eyeing his father. "Us as well? I don't take your meaning."

I find it interesting that neither Veseo nor Nouille has attempted to hug their father, or to

even look particularly happy to see him. I get
the feeling they aren't close and never were?

"And why the fuck are you laughing at us?"
Veseo says, trying to look put out. He can't
hide his smile though. He almost never remains
upset for more than a minute or two.

"You've managed to tie yourselves to a
Chosen, as well," Veles explains. "I thought I'd
seen it all when Herrick, Reve, and Malvolo
managed to find a mate in the omnifarious."

I recognize the names. During our travels,
Veseo spoke of his brothers often. He spoke of
Malvolo a little sadly, wondering often if he'd
been one of the bodies I'd been unable to raise.
He's Veseo's opposite. Quarrelsome and
discontent when Veseo is all smiles. They
argued constantly, which Nouille tells me is a
sign they cared deeply for each other.

Veseo and Nouille exchange a glance, faces
shining with hope. "They're alive?" Veseo
asks.

Veles nods. "They're staying with
huntsmen for the time being. If you fly to them
in the next few days, you may be able to catch
them, before they depart."

Both brothers turn to face me expectantly.
They're asking me to make the decision. And

I'm not comfortable with this resting on my shoulders. It's not my decision to make. Their brothers are alive and happy, of course they should go to them!

"I must raise the Blue Faerie," I say with a frown.

"We won't leave your side, Briar," Nouille says.

"But your brothers are alive," I start.

Veseo shakes his head. "And seeing them can wait until you do what you're meant to do."

I take a deep breath as I consider that. My necromancy still needs refinement. I don't really wish to bind the Blue Fairie to Payne, as well. It could get... awkward.

"Speaking of," Maura interjects with a cough. "We still need her raised."

"Tomorrow evening," I say, glancing at the window. The sky is lightening to gray. "It will be dawn soon and we need rest."

Maura nods. "Very well. Before the clock strikes twelve. There are chambers beneath the tower, if you'd like them."

I grin inwardly. Dusk will come hours before midnight. We'll be alone in our own quarters before the meeting need occur. We have time and that means possibilities.

"Yes, faerie godmother," I say innocently. "We'll be there."

***

Veseo shifts uncomfortably, wings flaring out slightly. He's unused to the straps that hold our supplies to his back. It will help me stay in place as well, creating a sort of saddle. The breeze from the motion ruffles my hair and I grin, patting one of his bronzed scales. It's almost as large as a plate and as reflective as glass. We've been traveling overland so long, I've almost forgotten what magnificent beasts they are.

Nouille will be unburdened, but for Payne, and he won't have to carry him for long.

He's agreed to join the Lost Boys in the port city of Anamore and purchase a sailing vessel. If what Maura suspects is true, he's the only one who can steer the boat to Tinkerbell's location.

"Not much longer," I say, giving Veseo and Nouille a reassuring smile before crossing over to Payne.

He jerks a little when I tap his shoulder, cranes his head to look at me, and then smiles. The expression is remote.

226

"What's made you so somber?" I ask, sliding a hand into his. He gives it an almost painful squeeze.

"I'm worried."

"Why?"

He shrugs. "Neverland is the literal end of the world. You topple off a waterfall into their damn ocean, for fuck's sake. I don't think it will kill me, but if it does..."

He slides his hand out of mine so he can sling a hand around my waist instead. He draws me in, tucks my head into the hollow of his throat. "You'll survive. Probably. And by that point you may have mastered your necromancy well enough to animate yourself and the others. Still…"

He glances at Nouille and Veseo, who wait patiently in what would have been the gardens in Bloodstone Castle. Everything is brown and lifeless. The vines long ago withered, the flowers just a memory, and even the shrubberies worn to defeated nubs. Maura has promised to stop pelting the land with acidic rains and extreme temperatures. Perhaps by the time the war is over, there will be a little green to return to. If we return at all.

"Don't tell the scaly bastards but they're alright. I'd sort of regret it if anything killed them."

I press my lips into a thin line, repressing laughter, especially when Veseo's long neck cranes down so he can bump his head against Payne's side. It's an almost cat-like move and it knocks Payne sideways. He's only just able to recover his feet.

"I think Veseo thinks you're alright too," I snicker, losing the battle. "And he'll probably be pissed if anything kills you, except him. Try to come back undead, alright?"

Payne nods. "That's the plan. Are you ready, Briar?"

Nerves assail me like a dozen stinging bees. I'm not sure I am. Honestly, one faerie should be easy after raising two dragons, right? This seems momentous. But, what if I bumble it?

I shrug off Payne's arm and cross over to the empty fountain where Maura has placed the Blue Fairie. Maura kneels over her, cursing any vines that grow too near her. She's needed to keep the Blue Faerie—Saxe, I hear she's called—under constant supervision. The ground wants to swallow the body whole and spawn new life. If that's what Saxe wants after she's revealed Tinkerbell's hiding place and the location of her lost wand, we'll lay her to rest someplace strategically beneficial, creating a barrier between Fantasia's forces and the forces of Morningstar.

My knees sting as they scrape the stone lip of the fountain. It's a relatively shallow bowl-shape that's streaked with grime from so many years of neglect. If I were Saxe, I think I'd be a little disappointed to wake in such a dreary place. Oh, well. Cadavers can't be choosers, I suppose.

Maura places a warm, reassuring hand on my forearm as I lean over Saxe's body. It's mostly been cleared of pixie dust, allowing me to see the cyan of her skin, and the silky fall of her teal hair. If it weren't for the stab wound under her left breast, she'd have looked like she simply fell asleep.

"I have faith in you, Briar. This is what you were born for," Maura says.

I didn't believe it. It was a random twist of fate that Zephyr had chosen me among the many children who'd been born during the war. Destiny doesn't dictate life. Determination does. I have to raise the Blue Faerie for the good of Fantasia. What happens after...

Who knows? When I'm trained, our place is on the front lines, taking the fight to Morningstar.

I brace my hands on either side of Saxe's head, screwing my eyes shut to blot out Maura's expectant stare. Full dark allows me to reach for my power all the more easily. Now that I know what is there and what to expect, it's easier to do it again. Just dip my hands into the cool like I am drawing from an arctic lake or river.

My fingers find the silk of her hair, wind into it and draw it up around her head so that I can cradle the back of her neck. Her flesh is cool against my skin, still thrumming quietly with power as her body tries to return to the earth from whence it came. In my mind's eye, I press her gently beneath the black surface of the water until she's submerged completely. The water floods into her nose, her mouth, drags her down, down, down, until...

Her body jerks, panicked like a woman who's woken to find she's drowning. She bats against the black lake until, finally, she comes alive, spitting and coughing. She jerks upright in my hands and I allow her hair to slide easily from my fingers. Her eyes fly open, revealing irises an indigo shade that's not much deeper than Payne's. A distant relation, at one point, perhaps?

They take a few moments to focus, like someone who has just woken from sleep. She raises a hand to scrub at one eye and pauses, spotting the glimmer of pixie dust on her skin.

"I'm dead," she murmurs. Her voice is high and trilling, a contrast to the almost sultry way Maura speaks.

"I'm afraid so," Maura says, leaning over the fallen faerie. "But you're back, at least for now."

Saxe doesn't cringe or recoil the way I expect her to. She just looks a little put out.

"You are a necromancer?" she asks, facing me.

I nod. "I am."

"Morningstar's people. Have they found the wand? Tinker's location?" she asks, her eyes drilling into mine.

"No, to both," I say. "Which is why you're here."

This time the Blue Faerie does jerk in surprise. Her skin pales to almost white.

"So... this is your doing, Princess," she says finally.

"This?" I ask, confused.

"I am in your power?" Saxe asks. "Beholden to you?"

I glance up at Maura, unsure of how to respond. "I... suppose. I don't intend to keep you under it, if you wish to go back to... wherever you were. We just need to know where you've taken Tinker. You hid her someplace in Neverland last time the war broke out and the Seelie were slaughtered. Well, the war is raging again and we need her. She's the last Seelie Fae in existence so she *has* to be the Chosen spoken of in the prophecies."

Saxe studies me. "I see. You must be Briar Rose."

"I am."

"You wake in a world you've never seen and involved in a war you had no say in. Are you sure you don't want to run?"

I squirm uncomfortably, recalling what Payne had told me about the Seelie Fae when we'd first met. Honest to the point of rude. Insightful as well, I suppose. It's a thought I've had many times during our journey. Woken to war, claimed by an enemy, bound to dragons. What a messy start to my strange unlife. Yes, I'm terrified of the coming confrontation.

232

Terrified I'll meet a painful end before I have a chance to truly live.

But, I have no choice.

"I'm not running," I say, glancing back at Nouille and Veseo.

Payne had climbed onto Nouille's back. He's got nothing but a length of cord to serve as reins. He won't be strapped in the way I will be. Being bucked off a dragon's back is more likely to be fatal to a fledgling necromancer than a decades-old vampire.

"No?" Saxe asks as I turn to face her again.

I shake my head. "There are things worth fighting for, Lady Saxe. And if I die? I won't be alone in the After."

Saxe follows my gaze and some of the cautious stiffness slides away. She studies them, then me, and finally lets out a breezy smile. It stirs the scrubby grass and shrubs like a summer wind.

"Alright. So we're clear... I've been dead a while and not everything makes sense to me just yet." She takes a deep breath. "Someone get me parchment. It appears I have maps to make."

EIGHTEEN
VESEO

The path leading to the House of Corvid is intentionally treacherous. Built primarily for bird shifters, the easiest pathway to it was to come in through the ceiling. While we *could* have flown over, neither of us were small enough to fit into the hole meant for avian shivers. At least, not since we were younglings. So, we approached using the footpath.

It had been made deliberately uneven so that it would take shifter dexterity to navigate without falling. Vanilla humans would be heard a mile off. Even with my reflexes, it is slow going, built like an obstacle course so that even I have to slow down to traverse it with Briar in my arms. Nouille walks just behind us, carrying Saxe, who has been attempting to hover for short periods of time, but exhausted herself.

Briar stares at the surrounding woods, a small scrunched line between her brows. The forest is pretty, especially under the light of a full moon, but I doubt she truly sees it.

"Payne will be fine," I murmur.

Briar's arms wound tightly around my neck as she adjusts her position. Her breath comes out shaky against my throat.

"We can't be sure of that," she whispers. "Maura told me about Neverland. It's brutal there, Veseo. They're at constant war. Even Peter didn't want to go back. Did you see the Lost Boys' faces when they were told? Poor Nibbles and Mayhaps cried."

"He'll be fine," I say, stressing the words for her benefit. "I'll never say it to his face, but he's a good man and a good soldier. They won't be there long. He'll bring back Tinkerbell."

"But…"

I raise a brow at her. "You said there were some things worth fighting for. Do you believe that?"

I can feel the heat of her blush against my skin and have to fight back a grin. Her soft skin looks incredible flushed pink with desire. If we have time before departing again, I'll compete with Nouille to see which of us can bring scarlet to those cheeks fastest. Nouille is surprisingly good at dirty talk, if prompted.

"Of course I do."

"Payne believes that, as well. He promised he'd come back to you. Have a little faith."

The treacherous obstacle course finally comes to an end, depositing us onto gently sloping ground. Waiting at the door for us is Vaughn Alden.

Alden is dark-skinned, with brown curls he keeps cut close to his skull. Easier to win in a brawl when your enemy doesn't have much to latch onto. His eyes are red-orange, betraying his heritage. He's a Gryphus Huntsman... or, at least, *was.* Shortly after his house defected, Alden renounced his oath, melted down his signet ring, and paid a professional to hack his wings off.

He'd gotten a handsome price for them, at some point and had used it to fund his own band of sellswords. He has no home to speak of, no loyalties except to certain huntsmen he still trusts, and no scruples when it comes to getting a job done.

Before we perished in the Battle of Nighburrow, my brothers and I were amused by tales told of him afar. He's gotten good at raiding tombs or breaking vaults to liberate treasures for his employers.

Which is exactly what we need now. Saxe can't recall where the wand was placed and we've received news that the wand is desperately needed to stop a plague Morningstar's generals are spreading through Sweetland. We're hoping Alden can decode the ciphers Saxe wrote or can find someone who will.

Vaughn doesn't crack a smile when we approach. He doesn't relax his posture or speak as he trails us with his eyes. He *does* remove his hand from the pommel of his sword, which is as warm a gesture as I've ever received from him. Alden, always read for battle, is assuring us we're welcome. It's a shame he'll stab me if I try to hug him.

Laconic and reserved, Alden rarely speaks. I suppose the sight of us must surprise him enough to prompt questions.

"I heard Princess Briar Rose was traveling with dead men," he says. His voice is like an aural avalanche, gravel and grit sliding into deep recesses. "I thought that meant vampires. This is a development. Do Malvolo and the others know you're alive?"

"No," Nouille says quietly. "But we'd like them to. May we pass? Saxe needs rest and

Briar would like to meet with Hattie and the others for training."

"And my mission?"

"Can wait a bloody hour," I grumble. "It seems like only weeks ago for us, but Mal, Herrick, and Reve haven't seen us in a decade or more. Let us pass or I'm going to go *through* you, Alden."

Alden's lips twitch just a fraction. You had to be looking to notice. He doesn't reach for his weapon.

"You think you can take me?"

I smirk. I can't help it. "I know I can. And it's hard to kill me, now that I'm dead, Alden. Think twice about starting a brawl."

He looks speculative and, though it doesn't show on his face, I know he's eager. He won't be leaving House Corvid until he's gotten a chance to spar with me. I'll admit I'm looking forward to the fight, myself. It's been so long since I've had a friendly bout with a worthy opponent. I won't be surprised if Malvolo doesn't get in on the action as well. The Mal I knew would never pass up an opportunity to brawl. Maybe marriage has mellowed him?

I snort. Malvolo, tied down to one woman? I won't believe it until I see it in person. The

Malvolo I remember, when not fighting in wars, filled his hours with whoring and collecting treasure and not necessarily in that order. He'd been as bad as our father. Though... given what I've seen at Maura's tower, it appears he's found a mate as well.

Veles, sire of the Southern Dragon Clan, tied to a fucking dark Fae. Now I *have* seen it all.

I have never been close to my father, but I will admit it was good to see him. And that's about all I'll admit on that subject.

Alden finally steps aside. "They'll be in the training rooms, I believe."

I incline my head gratefully to him and step through into the main hall. It's made of shining oak and decorated here and there with inlaid carvings of rooks, ravens, jays, crows, and more. Each of them has a name and date scrawled beneath it. They are the names of past huntsmen and women who died well, who died with honor. If we travel to House Accipitrine, I expect we'll find Peregrine's name on the wall there.

Most of the room is dominated by a hearth large enough to span most of my body. It's

currently lit and the room is hot enough that
sweat pops along my brow in seconds.

"Why is it so blazing hot?" I wonder.

Alden sidles up close and nods toward a
glass case in the corner. A young man in his
prime, with dark hair and an angular face is laid
out on blue velvet. His eyes are closed.

"For the Prince. Delerood is warmer than
these woods, most days. Mistresses Neva and
Carmine thought he'd prefer the heat."

"Oh, Gods," Briar breathes. She bats at my
arm and I set her down on her feet. She crosses
to the case, pressing her hands flat against the
glass. "He's like I was. Spelled asleep."

"So he needs to be snogged?" I ask.

Briar tugs her lip between her teeth. She
does that when she's indecisive and it's always
damn distracting.

The moment we're alone together, I'm
going to fuck that hot little mouth, the way I
had in Maura's underground chambers. I'll
have her anyway she'll allow, but Gods, her
mouth is amazing. Less need for oxygen and a
repressed gag reflex make for phenomenal
blow jobs.

"No, I think... I think I can wake him."

She glances up at us uncertainly through thick lashes.

"You can wake him? But, he's not dead?"

She nods. "I know you want to see your brothers but... Would you mind if I stayed to try? Saxe will be here to help."

Nouille and I exchange a glance. I'm torn. Leaving Briar alone for any length of time feels like trying to remove a limb. On the other hand, my brothers aren't far away and it feels like I'm going to burst out of my skin if I don't see for myself that they're whole and happy.

"She'll be fine, Veseo," Nouille says quietly, wrapping long fingers around my wrist, tugging gently in the direction of the adjoining hall. "She's in the House of Corvid. She's as safe as we can make her."

He's right. The enemy will be hard pressed to steal her from a houseful of Huntsmen. It doesn't totally erase the worry, but I take a step back. She seems intent on trying to wake the prince. If she can do something for him, I should let her. Delerood was and is our ally in this war.

Alden leads us toward the training rooms. I crane my neck to watch Briar for as long as architecture will allow and am momentarily

242

panicked when the bend of the hall hides her from my sight. Veseo, the cheerful jester of the Southern Dragon Clan reduced to wringing his hands like a fishwife when his woman is out of sight. Malvolo will laugh himself sick.

Sounds filter to us from the open door of the training room. A shaft of silver light filters into the hall. A woman's voice shouts encouragements from the sidelines, punctuated occasionally with cheers.

"It's not even fair," Reve's voice says, light and amused. "Go easy on him, Mal."

"Thanks for your vote of confidence," Herrick huffs. "It really warms my heart, brother."

Alden pauses in the doorway, blocking most of our view of the room beyond. The glimpses I catch are enough.

Herrick stumbles back a few steps before regaining his feet. The floor is dirt here, as the wood has been pied up to form a sort of pit. Herrick is dressed in the loose clothing huntsmen train in and he's filthy. It's concentrated on the back of his pant legs, the elbows of the shirt and in his upswept hair. Malvolo must have been kicking him into the dirt for hours.

As we watch, a booted foot gets past Herrick's guard and slams solidly into his chest, taking him off his feet. He skids to the very edge of the pit where Reve and a slender, dark-haired woman sit, legs dangling into the pit below. She beams at him, as though he hasn't just had his ass thoroughly handed to him.

"I'll kiss it all better later," she promises with a wink. She plants a soft, chaste kiss to his cheek anyway.

Malvolo appears in the gap next, sweat slicking loose hair to his brow, his chest heaving with exertion. He's still grinning.

"That was five, Herrick. I sleep in the bed with Neva. Again. This is why you keep up with your drills, brother."

"Next time," Herrick pants.

Alden waits until the bickering has died down to clear his throat. The occupants of the room turn in unison to look at him.

"Pardon, General. But Princess Briar Rose has arrived and she thinks you may want to see two members of her retinue."

He swings aside like he's a second, heavy door to reveal Nouille and I gawking like idiots. For a few seconds, we're all frozen in

244

place, staring at each other. Emotion crackles through the air, palpable even though none of us have as much as twitched, let alone spoken to each other. It's so fucking good to see them again. For weeks I'd wondered which of my brothers were in the grave with us. Even after learning the truth from father, I hadn't been sure how I'd react to seeing them.

It must be worse for them. What's weeks for us has been years to them. Enough time to grieve, for the wound to scab over and remain only an occasional throb. Our appearance must rip the scar tissue open, introducing the pain afresh. Malvolo's body has locked down, hands clenched into fists, eyes wide and unsure. Reve looks concussed.

There are tears in Herrick's eyes and he's the one who moves first, climbing to his feet in a motion so fluid, human eyes would be unable to follow. Then he's hurling himself at Nouille, who tries and fails to catch him. They both go down, hitting the floor with an audible clatter which seems to unfreeze Reve and Malvolo. They're still not speaking, staggering forward like drunks.

"What?" I say, throwing Malvolo the smirk he so hates. "No greeting for your brothers?"

"Veseo, you prick," Malvolo breathes.

Then he hurls himself at me. I'm better prepared than Nouille, bracing my back against the wall as both Reve and Malvolo crash into me. It's a good thing I no longer need to breathe, because Malvolo seems intent on crushing me. He throws his arms around me and squeezes so tightly, I'm afraid I'll experience my second death.

"Get off me, you muscle head," I say, shoving at his chest after a minute has passed. "I'm not Herrick. I've not let time turn me to flab!"

"Hey!"

Malvolo chuckles and releases me, allowing Reve to have a turn, and then finally, Herrick. In the end they form a semi-circle of beaming faces around us. Even Mal can't disguise the fact that he's giddy. I'll tease him about it later. I think they might have stayed like that for longer if the slender woman hadn't come to hover behind them. At some unspoken signal, they part and allow her into the circle. She wedges herself between Malvolo and Herrick, but they all end up touching her somehow. It reminds me of the groupings

Nouille, Payne, and I stand in so we can all keep contact with Briar.

They really are bonded to this Chosen. Well, I'll be damned.

"Who is this?" the woman asks, aiming the question at Reve, who appears to be the calmest of the three.

"Veseo and Nouille of the Southern Dragon Clan. Younger than Herrick and Malvolo, but older than me."

"Your brothers? They're alive!" She stares at us with newfound awe. She really is stunning. Sable hair, luminous amber-gold eyes, pale skin, and lush proportions. I can see at least part of the reason they're smitten. "I thought they died during the war."

"We thought so too," Reve says with a frown.

"If you've been out there this whole time, I'm going to gut you," Malvolo says with a trademark growl. My smile widens. Now *that's* the Malvolo I remember.

"We *are* dead," Nouille says and I can see the shock and confusion on my brothers' faces. "But Briar brought us back. She tried for all four of us but... Maug and Choro weren't able to be raised."

"May they rest in peace," Herrick says.

The rest of us nod and grow silent for a few seconds. It's Mal who breaks the silence.

"Then Briar is a necromancer?" he asks.

I nod. "She's in the hall, if you'd like to meet her."

"She's sort of..." Nouille trails off, coloring a little. He's no longer capable of the cranberry-red blushes he used to be known for.

"Ours," I finish for him. "So don't get ideas." I direct that statement to Malvolo.

Reve smirks and pats the woman's ass. "I'm sure Briar is lovely, but we're good, thank you."

"And I'm good with all three of you," the woman exclaims as she looks between them.

They laugh and latch onto a portion of her, following us back down the hall toward the main hall. We've just rounded the corner when there's a clatter of breaking glass and a man's shout. I go for the dagger tucked into my belt and see Malvolo do the same with the longsword at his waist.

All I can think about is Briar as I hope nothing's happened to her. Gods, if something has...

When we turn the corner, we don't find an assassin attempting to cut down the Blue Faerie or Briar. Instead, we see a young man in the jumble of shards, trying not to cut himself to ribbons. He looks almost as discomposed as I felt upon waking to the world again.

Prince Andric's chest heaves, panic shows in his eyes, but he manages to rise into a fighting position. Fisticuffs with a group of dragons seems pointless, but I applaud the courage it takes to make the attempt. His voice comes out raspy from disuse and he doesn't ask the question I'm expecting.

"Where the fuck is Aria?"

~

To Be Continued in
TINKER

Now Available!

DOWNLOAD FREE EBOOKS!
It's as easy as:

1. Visit my website (hpmallory.com)

2. Sign up in the popup box or the link on
the home page

3. Check your email!

HP MALLORY is a New York Times and USA Today Bestselling Author!

She lives in Southern California with her son, where she is at work on her next book.

Printed in Great Britain
by Amazon